Love, Jamie
Bought and Paid For

LOVE, JAMIE

AKM MILES

Love, Jamie
ISBN # 978-1-907010-87-3
©Copyright AKM Miles 2009
Cover Art by Natalie Winters ©Copyright 2009
Interior text design by Claire Siemaszkiewicz
Total-E-Bound Publishing

This is a work of fiction. All characters, places and events are from the author's imagination and should not be confused with fact. Any resemblance to persons, living or dead, events or places is purely coincidental.

All rights reserved. No part of this publication may be reproduced in any material form, whether by printing, photocopying, scanning or otherwise without the written permission of the publisher, Total-E-Bound Publishing.

Applications should be addressed in the first instance, in writing, to Total-E-Bound Publishing. Unauthorised or restricted acts in relation to this publication may result in civil proceedings and/or criminal prosecution.
The author and illustrator have asserted their respective rights under the Copyright Designs and Patents Acts 1988 (as amended) to be identified as the author of this book and illustrator of the artwork.

Published in 2009 by Total-E-Bound Publishing, Faldingworth Road, Spridlington, Market Rasen, Lincolnshire, LN8 2DE, UK. No part of this book may be reproduced, scanned, or distributed in any printed or electronic form without permission. Please do not participate in or encourage piracy of copyrighted materials in violation of the authors' rights. Purchase only authorised copies. Total-E-Bound Publishing is an imprint of Total-E-Ntwined Limited.

If you purchased this book without a cover you should be aware that this book is stolen property. It was reported as "unsold and destroyed" to the publisher and neither the author nor the publisher has received any payment for this "stripped book".

Manufactured in the USA.

LOVE, JAMIE

Dedication

To Mom, for being cool enough, at 82, to love what I'm doing and be proud of my successes.

Chapter One

"Somebody get me Jamie. Quick. I need help with Mr. Jenson in twelve-B," Nurse Betty yelled, trying to hold on to the large man who'd just managed to slide off the shower seat as he was attempting to get up. He didn't appear to be hurt, since he was laughing at his predicament, but they both knew that she wouldn't be able to lift him. He'd been in the centre for weeks and was due to leave soon but was still a little unsteady on his new knee.

A tinny voice came over the speaker on her waist. "I'll send for him right away, Betty. Hold on."

"Mr. Jenson, we'll have help in minutes. Jamie's great. He'll…"

"Don't worry. I know Jamie. I'm fine. It was my fault. I should have held on better." He chuckled and added, "I'm trying really hard not to be embarrassed. I'm sure I look ridiculous."

"Not at all," Betty started but had to stop and chuckle herself. He was wedged down between the seat and the side of the tub. He did look a little like a beached whale. He'd done so well lately that he'd been moved into the apartment area where there were tubs instead of walk in showers.

She heard Jamie coming in the door of the apartment and smiled gratefully.

"Hi, guys. Somebody said you needed help in here." Jamie smiled as he took quick stock of the situation.

"This looks like being caught between the rock and the hard place."

"It is pretty silly, huh?" Mr. Jenson smiled back at him. "Wanna help me up so I can get a little dignity back?"

"I can help you up, but I'm not sure about the dignity part." Jamie couldn't help teasing the man. They'd built up a nice joking relationship since Mr. Jenson had been here so he knew he wasn't gonna piss him off.

"Fine, Smarty. Just get me up so I can get dressed," Mr. Jenson muttered, red-faced, but still smiling.

"Betty, you can go on. I'll handle this from here. No problem." Jamie sent Betty away so he could get Mr. Jenson up from his current position, which couldn't be comfortable. He made sure that Mr. Jenson's knee was at the right angle so he wouldn't hurt it on the way up and he put his arms under the man's armpits and bent his knees and lifted. Mr. Jenson put his arms over Jamie's shoulders, and when he got part way up, he used his other leg to help, and soon, he was out of the tub onto the mat beside it. Jamie held onto him for a few seconds while he got his bearings.

Jamie turned Mr. Jenson to the toilet seat and eased him down, then handed him a bath towel. He checked to make sure that the man's clothes were nearby then stepped out of the small bathroom and waited for Mr. Jenson to call if he needed help. His cane was the bathroom with him so Jamie felt sure he would be okay.

In minutes, Mr. Jenson came out, fully dressed and only limping a little as he manoeuvred with the cane.

"Thanks, Jamie. I appreciate it. My hand slipped on the rail and down I went. When I pulled the cord, I was hoping you'd be the one to come, but poor Nurse Betty got the eyeful instead. Bless her heart. I'll be more careful in the future, believe me," he ended ruefully. He blushed again, obviously thinking of the picture he'd made.

"Hey, no problem. Betty's totally professional and capable. And as for me, well, it's what I'm here for. You good now? Need anything?"

"Nah, I'm good. I'm supposed to be making a bowl of soup and a sandwich for lunch in the little kitchenette thing over there. I'll try not to burn the place down." Mr. Jenson headed over to his next task, and Jamie headed back to Four Hall.

He'd been working with Miss Wilhemina when he'd been called away. Now, he hurried back to her room. He loved working with the dear old lady. She was ninety-eight years young. She was the oldest person he'd worked with to date, and he liked her immensely. She'd fallen in the assisted living home where she lived and broken her hip so she was here for some therapy and training before she went back.

"Is that you back already, dear boy?" she said, in that quiet voice of hers.

"Yes, ma'am. A patient fell and needed help getting up. He's fine, though."

"Well, that's good. Are you sure you have time to take me down to therapy?" she asked in a voice that told him she was afraid she was being a bother. Not.

"You're my number one priority right now, Miss Wilhemina, don't you worry. I'm right where I'm supposed to be. Here now, let me help you into the chair. How's the hip today?"

"Tolerable, dear. I expect it to hurt, so I guess it's doing right what it's supposed to." She had a way of looking at things.

"Not hurting too badly is it, though?" Jamie asked. She wasn't one to complain, but he wanted her pain managed if she needed it.

"Oh, shush. I'm fine. Now after I get back from the torture session, I may be singin' a different tune."

"Honey, I've told you that you should get a little something for pain before you go so it won't be so bad for you." It was a common practice to give patients something light to help ease them through the painful motions they would have to endure to heal the joint. Most patients wanted it, demanded it even. Miss Wilhemina was somewhat of a stoic. She could handle it, she always said.

"If I need something when I come back, I'll ask, okay?" She looked up at him as he unlocked the wheels on her wheelchair then rolled her out the door to the gym.

"Okay, darlin'. I just don't want you to hurt any more than you have to."

"You're a sweetheart. Hey, speakin' of...you got a sweetheart?" she asked, as they passed the cafeteria.

"No, ma'am. I'm too busy here and taking classes to think about anything else." Jamie was going to night school to get certified in physical therapy. He worked as a tech now, just to make ends meet, and it was the best training he could get.

"Well, don't let too much time go by. Enjoy love while you're still young," Miss Wilhemina advised.

Jamie didn't feel it necessary to inform her that if he did have a sweetheart it wouldn't be the sweet young girl she imagined. No, he was definitely for guys, but if anyone here knew about it, Jamie wasn't aware of it. He'd certainly never said anything, preferring to keep that part of his life totally separate. Not that there was much going on in that part of his life, for sure. He couldn't remember the last date he'd gone on. He hadn't even been to a bar or out with friends in...way too long, come to think of it.

The only other gay person he knew here was Donnie Wilkins, and he avoided Donnie like the plague. Donnie was the son of the man who owned this rehab facility. Jamie just didn't like him. Donnie had latched onto Jamie right after he'd started working here a couple of years ago and he acted like there was something between them, but there so wasn't.

Jamie went out of his way to stay off of Donnie's radar. Donnie acted like they were in a brotherhood or something. Jamie didn't even know how Donnie knew he was gay. He'd never seen Donnie at a bar or with anyone. Jamie had certainly never said anything, but Donnie had made remarks several times that made Jamie nervous—not that he was afraid of him, by any means.

Jamie was almost six and a half feet tall with well-defined muscles. He'd played ball in high school and liked being in good shape. It was hard to ignore him with his height, weight, and good looks. At least that's what he'd been told all his life. Blond hair, cut short on the sides, a little thicker on top, blue eyes, lush lips, tight round ass, nice package. He had it all. He was just too busy to take advantage of it. And really, he wasn't the type to take advantage of anything. Jamie was just, as the ladies here put it, 'a nice young man'.

He was fine with that. He had no aspirations towards being a stud or cool or a playboy. There was no doubt he could walk into any bar in town and walk out with anyone he chose. He just didn't play that scene, having been there, tried that, and not liked it. Having been on his own since he was eighteen, he was used to making his own choices. He just felt he made better choices these days.

Jamie liked working with the people who came here for healing. There were a lot of elderly, because they often fell and broke hips or needed either knee or hip replacements. Next, there were a lot of sports injuries with two colleges in the city with lots of teams, not to mention the park systems. Then there were the occasional injuries from falls, car wrecks, or job-related injuries. There weren't a lot of young people here as a rule, but there had been on occasion. He liked working with the youngsters as much as he liked his little old ladies. His LOLs he called them to himself. They loved him, Lord knew.

His reputation with the elderly ladies was well-known here. They considered him a sweetheart, which he didn't mind. They were fun. He treated them like gold, and they blossomed for him. It was easy to make them feel special by complimenting them and flirting a little, whatever they needed to lift their spirits. He found that older people often needed their spirits lifted. They'd lost people—spouses, friends, and family. He was saddened by their stories and did his best to make their rehab time a little brighter. It didn't hurt him, and he truly got joy from their smiles and the twinkle in their eyes.

After dropping off Miss Wilhemina, Jamie turned the corner coming out of the gym area and nearly ran into Jackie Harper, one of his best friends at the facility.

"Hey, Jack, what's up? You're in a hurry," he said, catching her arms so she didn't go down.

"We've got a new one, Jamie. It's bad." She looked a little frantic.

"How bad?" he asked and turned to follow her as she hurried down the hall.

"Really bad. Multiple injuries from a car wreck. He's got a broken collarbone and hip, torn muscles in his groin, broken ankle, and torn cartilage in same knee for us to worry about. 'Course there's lots of other minor stuff. But Jamie, he's a young coach, former basketball player and a real athlete. Oh and he's drop dead gorgeous under all those bruises."

"How can you tell if he's so bruised up?" Jamie asked, keeping pace with her rapid steps. With his long legs it was no problem keeping up with her little running steps. Jackie always seemed to be running, probably to make up for her short little legs. She barely topped out at five feet tall.

She glanced over at him and went on. "The bones aren't hidden by the bruises. He's a real looker. They sent me to find you. They're gonna need you. We're short on Three, and he's pretty...uh...resistant to help.

He could use your help and your strength...in more ways than one."

"Now Jack, I'll be glad to help but don't expect me to try any of your psychology stuff on him," he teased her. Jackie worked in the counselling area and did a great job with helping patients face the problems they were dealing with at the centre and with the rest of their lives.

"He needs...a lot of help, Jamie. Wait 'til you see him. He'll be here for a good while."

They'd traversed half the facility and were now slowing before room three-twelve. Just before they walked in they heard a low growl from inside.

"Please, just get out. Please. Just for a little bit." The voice was gravely and deep with a sense of desperation in it.

Jamie stepped back as one of the nurses and another tech came out, followed by one of the intake staff. Looked like the guy had gotten his fill of welcome. Jackie stood back and motioned Jamie in. He hesitated, and she pointed again for him to go in. He went.

"Hey, I'm Jamie," he said as he stepped into the room. Damn. The man was trussed up like —

Jamie couldn't even come up with a euphemism. The man's leg was raised and held immobile by a pulley system holding a canvas bag-like contraption. It kept his leg off the bed without binding it. He had dressings on his shoulder, and his arm was bruised from under the bandage down past the elbow. His chest was black and blue and surely it hurt him to breathe. Due to the leg being raised the man's privates were left in full view. Now hell, there was no reason for that. There was a large white dressing on his thigh and up to his hip. Ah, the torn groin muscle. Damn again.

"Now what?" the voice was resigned. The eyes were blue, really blue, almost like Jamie's. It was strange, since the man's hair was black, very straight, and kind of long, compared to Jamie's. Odd colouring. The right side of his face and neck was still bruised, but Jackie was right. Jamie's heart thudded. He saw what Jackie meant about the bones now. This man was gorgeous, definitely gorgeous. Those cheekbones were model material. His mouth was the stuff of dreams. Women paid a lot to get lips to look that full. He'd love to see what they felt like against his own. Whew. Straighten up, now. Well, at least get serious. He couldn't get straight.

"Oh, hey, I don't want anything. I'm here to see if I can help in any way. First, let me get a sheet pulled over a little so you won't be flashing the public. Figure you might appreciate that." Jamie went over and grabbed the sheet someone had left lying on the other side of the man and eased it over the top of him, restoring his modesty.

"One thing you learn when you're in the hospital for a while is that modesty goes out the window, but I appreciate it, man. Thanks." The man tried to move a little to ease an ache or something but winced at even the slightest motion. Ouch. Poor guy.

"No problem. Can I get you anything? A drink of water? Are they finished with you for a while? Do you want to nap a little before the next wave hits with their own list of annoying questions and proddings?" Jamie knew what it was like. Every area of the facility had to get their info on him so they'd be ready to work with him in their own way when necessary, but it was a pain in the butt for sure.

The patient chuckled and sighed a little. "Yeah, I could use a nap. I don't sleep for more than a few minutes at a time anymore anyway. I'm always so tired. I'm Grant...Grant Stevens." Grant's voice began to slur a little as he headed towards oblivion.

Jamie found himself wanting to smooth the hair off Grant's forehead. Just to feel how soft it was. Someone must have washed it before he'd left the hospital to come here. It was shiny and looked like it would feel like silk. Jamie shook his head at himself. That would be just what he needed. To get caught caressing the new patient while he slept. Lord help him.

Jamie checked to make sure Grant had ice water and the kit everyone received upon admittance. Yep, all there. He headed out, but stopped at a gasp from behind him.

He turned and saw that Grant was awake again and looked scared for a moment. Jamie hurried back to the head of the bed.

"It's okay, Grant. Relax. Shh," Without thought, his hand went up, and he smoothed the hair off Grant's forehead. He drew back his hand as if he'd touched fire. Idiot. What was he doing? His instinct had been to comfort. He looked quickly at Grant to see if he was furious or pissed, but his eyes were closed again. Whew. Jamie started out again, but when he did, Grant whimpered. There was no other word for it. When Jamie turned again Grant's eyes were open and filled with pain.

"Grant, are you in a lot of pain? I can get the nurse for you. They'll get you something."

"No…gave me something when I got here…I just don't want to…" He stopped and closed his eyes again. It looked like he was going to sleep whether he wanted to or not. Jamie started to ease away, and again there was a sound from the bed. He slipped back over, and while every muscle in his body screamed at him to touch the man, to ease him, he was afraid to follow through. What if it was misconstrued? He could do that with his LOLs 'cause they ate it up and it made them feel better and he knew it was okay with them. But this was a young, strong, vital man. It wouldn't be the same. It was better to leave.

He headed for the door and heard what almost sounded like a sob from behind him. He couldn't do it. He couldn't leave the man in such pain without trying to help him. He turned back and went to the head of the bed again.

"What do you need?" Jamie put his hand gently on the shoulder that wasn't trussed up.

"I don't know…I just feel better with you in here. I've…I've never been this way…I feel like a fool…weak…whiny…wimpy…so…so not…like me." Grant looked into Jamie's eyes, his own full of tears he couldn't even reach up and clear away. "It scares me," he finally admitted.

"I understand. No, I do." Jamie said as Grant looked sceptical. Jamie took a tissue and smoothed away any evidence of Grant's tears. He knew Grant wouldn't want signs of weakness to be seen by others.

"You do?"

Jamie went on to explain. "Your body's betraying you. You're used to being strong and healthy and in command of it. Now it's letting you down. You're weak and shaky and in pain and scared. Trust me, I know. I've seen it over and over."

Grant had looked almost angry at Jamie's words but began to listen and pay attention.

"It's the trauma your body's been through. You're going to get it back. The physical therapists here are fabulous. You'll soon hate them, but by the time you leave, you'll hug them all." Jamie assured him

Jamie walked around the bed. Grant's eyes followed him, taking it all in. "The first little while is for building up your strength to where you can handle the torture they're going to put you through. Then you go to work, man, and it will be gruelling." Jamie didn't lie to people, and he especially couldn't to Grant. He liked this guy. He felt something for him specifically. He'd be smart and never admit it, but he did. He promised himself he'd figure these feelings out later, but right now, Grant needed to relax and believe.

Grant asked, "What do you do here?"

"I'm just a tech. I'll help with moving you since you're a big guy and I always get called to help with big ones since I'm such a hulk myself. I may bring your food. I may empty your bedpan. I may help you bathe. Whatever is needed, I do. It's up to you. If you'd be more comfortable with a female tech, I'll arrange it, but I'll probably be around for the heavy lifting." He didn't want to make Grant uncomfortable.

"No, please. I'd be more comfortable with you than a female tech or whatever. I hate this, being weak and needing someone to do the littlest thing for me. It's…" Grant paused, looking for the right word.

"Demoralising? Humiliating? Degrading?" Jamie supplied some of the many he'd heard. It was all true, but necessary right now. "I know. I can only promise it will get better. I swear I'll help. Now, will you close your eyes for a while and rest before respiratory gets here, then they'll come for some of your blood, then — you get the picture?" He winked at Grant.

"Yeah. SSDD."

Jamie laughed. Grant was right. *Same Shit, Different Day.* It was obvious he knew the program all right. He stopped pacing, stood beside the bed and looked at Grant for a minute.

"Need anything?" he asked, seriously.

"Nah." Grant yawned and winced as it pulled against his jaw that was still a little blue. Jamie almost reached out to him. He put both hands behind his back. He wanted to touch Grant's hair again and smooth his neck there where it joined his shoulder. Slide his fingers on down and feel that taut chest, check out the abs under the cover. His mind followed his hand downward to discover the interesting bulge between Grant's legs.

Jamie made himself snap out of his reverie. He would have to be careful. He couldn't be his normal self with this guy. Older people and young kids needed to be touched. This guy might just get him fired. He stood a few minutes and watched as Grant finally succumbed to sleep then slipped out.

"So is he as hot as they say?"

Jamie nearly jumped out of his skin as the voice came from behind him when he stepped outside Grant's door. Hell. Donnie.

"Damn, Donnie, quit creepin' around."

"So? I hear he's a hunk? You hot for him?" Donnie was getting just a little too pointed with his questions. Had he seen Jamie touch Grant's hair? God help him if Donnie ever had any ammunition against him. The man was such a sneak. He wanted something on Jamie, and Jamie knew it.

"What do you want? I've got to go back to Four Hall."

"I just wanted to see our new celebrity. Hear he was a hotshot coach, but now, he's cracked up and wasted."

"You have such a way with words and so much compassion. He'll be fine." Jamie wasn't going to discuss Grant with Donnie. No way. He didn't want the two together in any way.

"Maybe I'll just go visit the man, welcome him to our facility. Be the right thing to do, don't ya think? Isn't that what you were doin'?" Donnie made it sound like Jamie had been doing something wrong.

"Man's sleeping, Donnie. Let him rest." Jamie shut up. He didn't want to seem like he was championing Grant.

He often wished he could just tell off Donnie and have done with it, but Donnie was the owner's son and didn't seem to have a real job. He was always around, in the way, and bugging the shit out of Jamie. Jamie liked everything about working here, except having to deal with Donnie. He actually got the willies around the man.

Turning, he found Donnie watching him, a calculating look on his face.

"You are hot for him, aren't you?" Donnie sneered.

"What are you talking about? I just met the man, asked if he needed anything and now I'm on my way to see if Miss Wilhemina is ready to go back to her room. What is your problem, and *what* are you implying?" Maybe it was time he had it out with Donnie. The man had never accused Jamie of anything, but he was always dropping little snide remarks about Jamie that made him nervous.

"I know about you, Jamie-boy." Donnie smiled like they shared some big secret.

"Spit it out. You know what about me?" Jamie's insides actually quivered, thinking he would be outed here at work and end up losing this job he loved. Donnie was just mean enough to do it, too. Being gay wouldn't necessarily lose the job for him, but Donnie would twist things around and make something ugly out of it. Jamie lived in fear of that.

"Why...you seem worried, Jamie? What's the matter? You afraid I'll tell what I know?" Donnie clearly enjoyed making Jamie squirm.

"If you've got something to say, say it. I've got work to do. I'm tired of these veiled threats you keep throwing out. What are you getting at, Donnie?" Jamie had had it with Donnie. Enough!

"Just that I've never seen you with a woman. You never hit on the nurses here, and I figure there's a reason for that."

That was it? That's what Donnie thought he had on him.

"Maybe because this is my job. I don't hit on my friends, and I doubt if you and I would hang out at the same places outside of here. So, are we finished?" Jamie was so tired of this. Donnie didn't have anything on him, just a hunch.

"We could...uh...hang out at the same places outside of here...if you know what I mean." Donnie got closer and Jamie felt that his space was not only invaded but tainted.

He backed up until he was against the wall beside Grant's room. "I'm so not interested. You're not my type. Sorry." Not really, but he threw it out there anyway.

"I'm not good enough for you, huh?" Donnie was getting loud.

Shit.

"I'm just not interested in anyone. I'm busy. Working and going to class takes up all my time. Nothing personal. I'm just not into anything else right now." Jamie hoped that was enough to get Donnie off his case and out of his sphere.

"Hmph. Sure, Jamie-boy. Sure." How did Donnie make that sound so threatening?

Donnie left. He turned and went back down the hall, leaving Jamie standing against the wall like a deer caught in the headlights.

"Jamie?" he heard a hesitant voice coming from Grant's room.

He shook himself and stood straight and headed back inside. He hoped Grant had not heard the conversation, but that would be too easy.

"Yeah? You need something?" Jamie asked as he came up close to Grant.

"Who was that, and why was he hassling you?" Grant's voice was sort of rough and low. He looked concerned.

"That was just Donnie, the owner's son. Don't worry about him." Jamie hated that he even had to talk about Donnie to Grant.

"I don't like him. He's trying to cause trouble for you. He wants you for himself, doesn't he?" Grant looked right at Jamie, waiting for an answer.

"Uh...I..." Jamie was speechless. It was true. Obviously, Donnie wanted Jamie and was pissed that Jamie wanted nothing to do with him. How was he to answer without admitting anything?

"It's okay. I'm not going to say anything to anyone. I don't care what you do in your time off. I just don't like seeing someone hassled. You don't have to say anything. I'm not asking anything personal." Grant looked right into Jamie's eyes and let him see he understood where Jamie was coming from and he didn't care. Jamie's shoulders slumped, and he relaxed a bit.

"Thanks. He's more or less stalked me since I started working here two years ago. He keeps getting just a little more obnoxious all the time. It's the only thing I hate about this job," Jamie admitted as if he and Grant had been friends forever.

"Dude sounds creepy."

"I'm sorry you had to hear all that. I shouldn't have confronted him anywhere near a patient's room," Jamie said, shrugging his shoulders a little and wishing the whole scene away.

"No problem. Takes my mind off my own miserable life." Grant smiled at him, and Jamie's heart thudded again. He really had to watch it around this guy. There was no doubt in his mind he could end up falling in a big way and that would not be a good thing.

As Jamie had predicted other groups started coming in to do their thing with Grant so he slipped out and went back to see about Miss Wilhemina. He got busy after that and ended up not seeing Grant again before the end of his shift. He was off the next two days so it was a while before he saw Grant again.

Chapter Two

Jamie tried not to wonder about Grant while he was off. He had work to do for classes and general house cleaning. He had a small house not too far from the centre. It was his parents' old house. He'd wanted to get out of his ratty apartment and had always wanted a house. He missed them, but he was happy with the memories here. He was happy to be back in it. He'd done a lot to brighten it up and added on a deck out back.

Now it was a nice little place. He'd worked his ass off. Traded work with friends to get things done at the house. He'd babysat, and dog sat, and even hauled in hay once to get some carpentry work done. It hadn't been too hard to find people who could either do things on the bartering system or who would be willing to teach him how to do it.

Well, he'd tried, but he had to admit as he went in the back door of the centre, that he had worried about Grant and how he was doing. His anxiousness to see

Grant again bothered him as he got his stuff settled and headed out to see what he needed to do.

Jamie was assigned to Three Hall today, Grant's hall. He tried to deny that his pulse raced a little. Quickly, he joined Jackie as she got out trays for lunch. She handed him three twelve as he came up to her. Fate, he thought. He pushed open the door and stepped into Grant's room.

"Hey, uh…Jamie, right? You disappeared on me."

Grant was smiling. Wow. What a difference a couple days made. He was still trussed up and hooked up to things, but he looked a little more comfortable.

"Yeah, sorry. I had a couple days off. Got some schoolwork done and some things around home. I have your lunch here. Oh, yummy, mystery meat and watery potatoes. Oh, and lime Jell-O. I can't say I envy you," Jamie teased.

"Oh boy."

"How's it goin'? You need help eating?"

"Nah, I'm clumsy with my other hand, but I can do it. I don't eat much of it anyway. Enough to not get yelled at, but…yuk, ya know?" Grant grimaced as the food was placed over his lap. Jamie cranked the bed up a little, being careful not to go too far as he watched Grant's face to make sure he wasn't causing him any pain. He caught a slight wince and stopped.

"Hey, I don't know if you've got a wife or family or friends who can do it, but you're allowed to have stuff brought in if you want. They don't say anything about it. Someone could bring you some real food."

"There's nobody," Grant said, bluntly.

"I can't believe that. You're a coach. You've got to have friends and people you work with and well, a team…and…I'll just shut up here 'cause it's none of my business. Sorry, I'll be back to get this in a bit and see if you need anything else."

"A bath maybe, later?" There was hope in Grant's voice.

"Sure, no problem." Jamie headed out to deliver more trays. He was going to be so professional. He *so* was. He wouldn't even allow himself to think about the fact that he would bathe Grant. It was something he'd done a million times for others, and it'd never fazed him. Wouldn't this time, either. Sure it would, but no one, Grant included, would know.

After all the trays had been returned, and he had attended to several other chores, he headed for Grant's room. Grant was to start on physical therapy tomorrow, and Jamie was sure the man was anxious. At the beginning, there would only be a few things for his good hand and coordination therapy until he was less restricted.

Right now, the man needed a bath.

Jamie entered the room to find Grant napping. He closed the door firmly and went to the sink, retrieving the pan and soaps from under it. He ran warm water in, got a cloth and a couple of towels and set them all on the tray table.

Grant was awake now and watching.

"Oh, hey. You ready to get clean?" Jamie asked, wringing out the cloth and soaping it. "How much can you do? I know you hate having to depend on others, but while it's embarrassing for you, it's just my job. We've all done this so many times, it's nothing. I'll let you do all you can by yourself without pain. I'll take care of the rest. Deal?" He waited to see what Grant would say.

"Yeah, thanks. I can do my face with my left hand and part of my neck and my chest a little, but then it pulls really bad. The woman yesterday didn't even give me the choice. It was…uh…not good."

Jamie could tell Grant was embarrassed.

"Oh, who was on yesterday? I don't remember. She wasn't rude, was she?" Jamie didn't believe in that. These people came in with pain and fear and anxiety over their futures, they didn't need their present any more stressful.

Grant looked at Jamie as he ran the cloth over his chin and neck and sighed a little at how good it felt. Jamie reached for it, swished it around in the pan and returned it.

"Nah, not really," Grant answered. "She just didn't bother to say anything. She flipped back the sheet and started scrubbing away."

"Dude, no way. Here, is that all you can reach? Let me take over and show you how it's supposed to be done." Jamie proceeded to give the man a thorough bath, not missing a thing, but being so matter of fact and straightforward about it that Grant didn't have a chance to be embarrassed. Jamie talked the whole time, asking about the upcoming therapy and telling little anecdotes about his work without mentioning names.

He had placed a towel over Grant's waist and hips as he finished with his arms, chest and stomach. He washed, he dried, he did the deodorant, and he even powdered a bit. He went to run clean water and washed out the cloth then returned to the bedside, talking all the while.

Jamie laid the towel aside and went on with washing Grant. Right now, and for a little while more, until the casts and slings and pain were gone, Grant would not be able to reach below his waist to take care of things, so Jamie made sure he was good and clean so he would not have to worry about it. Grant could only move the one leg a little for Jamie to get between there, but Jamie was gentle and made sure he wasn't hurting Grant as he took care of business.

All the while, he caught quick little glances at Grant's face to make sure he was okay. Sometimes, this was the worst part for people. Some folks were really shy and hated being touched in this personal way. Jamie tried to make it as impersonal as possible, as if it was no big deal.

Grant answered his questions when it was necessary, but kept his eyes closed most of the time. He seemed to appreciate the way Jamie worked quickly and efficiently but compassionately. When the bath was over, a new sheet was over him and Jamie cleaned things at the sink, Grant sighed.

"That felt wonderful," he said quietly. "I feel better than I have since I got here. You're a good guy, Jamie. You didn't make me feel like a slab of meat, but you didn't make me want to die of embarrassment, either. Believe me, I've felt both ways since this all started. I...uh...appreciate it, really."

"No problem."

Grant chuckled a little and added, "And no one else has powdered me."

"Hey, my LOLs love it. I know the sheets get rough and you get tired of laying on them and any little bit of pampering helps. I'm just so used to that being part of the routine that I did it without thinking. I won't again if it bothers you." Jamie really hadn't thought about it.

"No, really. You're right. It feels good, and it makes sense, and what are LOLs?" Grant asked, smiling now.

"Shh. That's what I call them. LOLs are my little old ladies. We have a lot of them here. Lots of broken hips, hip replacements, knee replacements, and so on." Jamie smiled as he talked about his elderly patients. "I love them. They're so sweet, and I enjoy helping them."

"I bet they love you," Grant teased.

"Yeah, I guess. They keep me hopping. I need to get going. You need anything? TV on?"

"No. Thanks. I'm good."

Jamie was busy all afternoon, going from room to room and answering call buttons. Refresh one lady's ice water, help one into the bathroom and wait for her to finish then help her back to the bed, take a couple to and from physical therapy, help out in the occupational therapy sessions for a couple of his ladies. It was a pretty normal day.

Every time he passed Grant's room, he peeked in to see if he was doing okay. Grant was not demanding at all. There were so many things he could be asking for and receiving, but he didn't ask for much. Jamie wondered about Grant's state of mind. He took a few minutes about a half hour before the time for supper trays to check on him.

"Hey, how's it goin' in here? You need to hold it down. The neighbours are complaining about the noise," he teased, as he went up to Grant.

"Hey."

Not a lot of feeling there, Jamie thought.

"What's up? You seem kinda low," Jamie asked, "Anything I can do?"

"Hell. I'm just having a pity party. Glad you stopped by. Maybe you could slap me into a better mood," Grant admitted.

"Well, I think the administration would frown on the slapping part, but I can try to cheer you up. Will you tell me something — and if it's none of my business, just tell me that, too."

"Go ahead and ask."

"I don't get it. You're young, good looking, a coach. Where are all the people who should be coming to visit you? I mean, women, kids from the team, your family? I know you're not alone. You can't be."

"Just as a matter of interest, why can't I?" Grant asked, cocking his head as he looked up at Jamie.

"I…well…I don't know. It just seems wrong." Jamie knew it was good for the morale of the patients to have visitors, loved ones, coming by to show support. Grant seemed like the kind of person who would have lots of people who cared for him. Where were they?

"Jamie, don't sweat it, okay? I'm basically a loner. I coach a couple hundred miles from here in Crandall. I don't have a wife or any other family. My team is on spring break so, frankly, no one knows about the accident. I was travelling alone when a drunk driver came across the median and ploughed into me, forcing my car into a van next to me. My car kind of became an accordion with me in the middle." Grant finished his story in a matter of fact voice that asked for no sympathy.

Jamie just wanted to give the man a hug. It sounded so sad to him, and he knew his thoughts were evident on his face.

"Wow." That was all he could say.

Grant grinned as he caught the look on Jamie's face. "I know you're the kind of person who just hates the thought of anyone being alone, but I've always been. Came up through the foster care system, went to college on a basketball scholarship, got my degree and became a coach. I'm used to being alone in my own time."

"Man, doesn't that suck?"

"When I'm coaching the team, I'm all theirs, and they know I'll do anything for them, but other than at school, I'm on my own. It's what I'm used to," Grant finished, obviously hoping Jamie would let it go and not probe further.

"Okay...I guess I get that. No wife, girlfriend, significant other?" Jamie asked before he could stop himself. Now he was getting personal.

"No, no, and uh...no," Grant said, raising his left hand before Jamie could go on. "I know that seems wrong to you, but it just seems normal to me."

"Dude, don't you get lonely? I mean, I live alone, too. But I have friends over, and I go out with them, and we eat out and catch movies and ballgames. Don't you miss being around people?" Jamie realised he was pushing too far, but he felt so bad for Grant. He just couldn't believe Grant was okay with things that way.

Grant was silent for a few seconds, and Jamie felt like he'd overstepped.

"Hey. Don't answer that. It's none of my business. I'm stickin' my nose in *yours,* and that is not acceptable. I'm sorry, Grant. Your life is your business, and I have no right to seem like I'm passing judgment on it. I should just leave," Jamie said, embarrassed as he realised how really pushy he'd been.

"Jamie, relax. It's okay," Grant said, motioning for him to sit in the chair by the bed. Jamie sat.

"By the way," Grant said. "That guy who was buggin' you the other day came by yesterday." He watched Jamie to see what he would say.

"No way. What did he want?" Jamie knew Donnie had no business in the patient's rooms.

"Actually he was asking about you. He seemed to think...well...he almost acted like he was jealous or something. Wanna fill me in on the situation there?" Grant kept close watch on Jamie's expression. "

"Good Lord. Donnie has no business in here, and certainly none talking to you about me. I can't stand the man. I told you the other day, he's been sort of trying to—I don't know how to say it. He's been trying to get close to me for the whole time I've been here. It started out as harmless and I ignored it, but then it began to get pointed."

"Sorry, but...creepy."

Jamie shrugged his shoulders. "I don't know what to do here. He's hinted that he could cause me problems with my job. He's the administrator's son."

"That's a threat. Can't you do something? He gives me the willies. I don't like the way he looked at me…and I don't even like the way he *talked* about you. He implied that you all were a couple."

Jamie jumped straight up, and it was all he could do not to scream out obscenities. The bastard! He turned and faced Grant, wanting him to understand and believe him "Grant, man, I'm sorry. That is so wrong. First, I'm not 'a couple' with anyone. I'm alone, as far as a love life goes. I can't stand Donnie Wilkins, never could. Frankly, he makes my skin crawl."

Grant kept close watch on Jamie's expression. "Relax. No harm done."

"He had no right to even come in here, much less to question you or try to intimidate you."

Jamie was almost in a state of shock. What was he going to do? He shook his head, trying to get his mind working.

"Hell, I had only been in here one time before today. What is he thinking? I'm going to have to put a stop to this. I can't tell you how sorry I am that he brought you into his little soap opera."

"Hey, it seems to me like it's not your fault. He's deluded maybe, huh?"

"Maybe, hell." Jamie didn't know what to think. Should he go to Mr. Wilkins. Would that make things worse? Should he try to talk to Donnie? He shuddered at that thought, but what else could he do?

"Listen, I'll arrange to stay out of here so…" Jamie started.

"No."

Well, that was blunt.

"No? I was just trying to think of you and keeping him out of your way."

"But then you'd be punishing me…to please him."

Jamie just looked at him. Punishing him? Uh, that would mean...uh, did he mean...?

"Why should I be deprived of your company and your help, just because he is..." Grant looked past Jamie to make sure no one was near before he finished, "full of shit?"

Jamie burst out laughing. Wonderful. That made him happy in a number of ways. Grant recognised that Donnie was a craphead, just like Jamie did. Grant thought it would be a punishment if Jamie was not there for him. Well, hey. He liked the sound of that. He liked Grant a lot.

"Damn. I've got to go get busy with the supper trays. I hear them coming down the hall. I'll bring yours, then do the others. I'll come back for yours last and maybe we can talk just a little more. I'm a little freaked out by this situation with Donnie. It bears thinking about."

"Go on. Don't worry about it. We'll figure something out."

Jamie felt warm from head to toe. Grant felt like it was the two of them against Donnie. Not just Jamie alone. 'Course Donnie had brought Grant into it. Grant could have gotten really pissed, though. For a man who spent his life alone, it seemed odd that he was aligning himself with Jamie.

An hour or so later, Jamie was back again. He grabbed Grant's tray and placed it into the cart and since he had arranged it so that was his last chore for a little while, he went back into Grant's room.

"My mind is just a mishmash of thoughts and worries right now. I admit I'm lost as to what would be the best thing to do. I'm just sorry you've been brought into the whole mess," Jamie began.

Grant waved Jamie over to the chair by the bed. "Okay, can we just get over that? Sit down and let's figure something out. Hey, it gives me something to think about instead of the pain I'm headed for tomorrow and the next few weeks. Don't worry about it. He's not gonna hurt me," he said, looking over at Jamie.

"He, by hell, better not."

"Now we have to figure out a way to keep him from hurting you."

Jamie said, "I wish he'd try, the smarmy little weasel. I could handle it if he tried something physical. He's not dumb enough to take me on. But he could mess with my job, as he's implied more than once. I just never worried about it, 'cause he never really pushed this far."

"Do you have any kind of rapport with the administrator himself, or is he just a boss? Could you go to him, confidentially? Or does he dote on Sonny?" Grant asked, taking the bull by the horns.

Jamie answered, "I've always gotten along with Bob, but we're not cohorts, so to speak. If you go by the way Donnie talks, dear old dad would do whatever he suggested. I think Bob is smarter than that, but if it came down to my word against his son's, I doubt if I'd win."

Jamie also would hate to run to the man and complain about Donnie's treatment of him.

"Yeah, and I can't see you going to him whining about Donnie bugging you. Not your style," Grant said, mentioning nearly the same thing Jamie had been thinking.

Jamie took a moment to feel good that Grant knew that about him after such a short acquaintance. It showed Grant had been thinking about him.

"You're right."

"So that leaves confronting Donnie or just ignoring him to see if he goes further. What do you think is better?" Grant asked, pitching the ball into Jamie's court.

"I'd love to just keep on ignoring him, but I can't ignore that he came here to hassle you. That's just not right. And, since I don't feel like it's right to punish you with my absence, I'm gonna have to do something." Jamie was brave enough to smile right into Grant's eyes, hoping he wasn't going too far.

"There is that." Grant smiled back.

Oh, don't go there, Jamie thought to himself. *Don't allow yourself to think that he might be interested in you. Just because he doesn't have a wife or girlfriend does not mean that he's gay.* But boy, could he dream!

"Listen, Grant. I'm gonna be spending more time with you in the next few days. You're starting PT, and I'm going to be lifting you from the bed to the chair and back. It's a special one, so your leg can stay straight for the time being." Jamie made a motion with his leg straightened out to show Grant what he meant. "I'm the one they'd call even if I wasn't working this hall. So, you're kinda stuck with me."

"Gee, that's the only good thing about this." Grant chuckled as he replied to that.

Jamie wondered what would happen if he just leaned over and planted one on Grant. He was beginning to crave that—just to bend a little and lay his lips on top of Grant's, pressure them open and take a taste. He wonder what Grant would do if he slid him a little tongue? Bite it off? Tangle his with it? Suck on it?

Jeeezus! Jamie decided he was losing it. The things Grant kept saying led Jamie to believe that he *might* be interested. He silently admonished himself again. *Don't even think it.* That would be mixing business and pleasure, and he couldn't afford to go there. But he could secretly wish he could. Oh yes, he could wish.

"Well, that being said, it looks like I'm going to have to see what Donnie is planning. I need to head out now and check on all the others. You need anything? You comfortable?"

"Well, no, actually. Is there any way you could help me scoot over a little. I'm getting kind of numb. I know I can't lie on my side, but if I could…"

"I've got just the thing. Here, wait a minute," Jamie said, going to the closet and reaching up for the extra pillow. He went back to Grant and very gently rolled him just a little and placed the pillow just under his back and hips so he was off his butt a little. He was pleased when he heard Grant sigh in relief.

"God, that's wonderful. Thanks. Just that little bit makes all the difference," Grant said to Jamie.

"No prob. It's my job to know these little tricks." Jamie patted Grant on his good shoulder. "I'm heading out. I'll check back before I get off later to see if you need anything."

"You gonna tuck me in?" Grant asked, then his eyes widened as if he was surprised by what he'd said. He almost looked scared, waiting for Jamie's reply.

Jamie decided to take pity on him and not push it. "I tuck in everybody."

He shrugged to himself as he headed out, thinking about the look of relief on Grant's face when he hadn't called him on the flirtatious question.

As he was working, Jamie spent some time thinking about Grant, if he was gay and whether he was out. Maybe that was the reason for the on then off way he had of speaking then doubting himself. Jamie didn't know what he hoped for. If the man *was* gay, Jamie had to admit he was more interested than he'd been in anyone in ages. If not, he was doomed to unrequited…uh…lust.

Well, he was used to that. He never had time to act on any interest he formed, anyway, so what else was new? What else? Grant was way more than he'd been interested in for a long time. Grant was special. Jamie didn't question that, he just knew that Grant was something else.

Jamie was on the lookout for Donnie the rest of the evening. He didn't look forward to seeing him, but he knew if he saw the man, he'd have to say something.

Donnie didn't work at the facility, but he always seemed to be hanging around. Jamie didn't know what he did, really. He didn't know if anyone did. On occasion, he'd heard others here talking about Donnie and wondering what he did for a living and why he was always hanging around.

He was walking down the hall when he saw the light over Miss Wilhemina's door come on. He hurried to see what she needed.

"Hi, sweetie, whatcha need?" he asked, as he eased to her bedside.

"Jamie, I'm gonna have to give in and admit that my hip is really hurting me tonight. I just can't seem to get restful," she admitted, sounding ticked off that she couldn't manage without pain meds.

"Honey, it's okay. Maybe you did just a little too much in therapy today and got it all fired up. I'll get the nurse, and we'll have you fixed up in no time. Anything else I can do for you? Pillows okay?" He looked to make sure they were arranged so she'd be off that hip and not get sores on her behind. At her age, her skin was fragile. Bed sores were a real problem.

"I'm fine, dear boy. Just did a little too much today, I guess. Thanks." She was always so mannerly and polite.

He wondered if he'd make a good patient if he were in as much pain and confined like his patients were. It was doubtful. While he had all the patience in the world with them, *he* was a mover, a doer. He had to be doing something all the time. That's probably why his patients loved him. He was always in and out and wasn't one for taking breaks and kicking back. He'd rather be visiting with them and helping them with little things when he wasn't involved with a major task. He'd hate having to be idle.

* * * *

The Donnie thing became a nonissue for the next several days. Donnie didn't make an appearance so Jamie quit looking for him and just did his job. As expected, he spent a lot of time shuttling Grant back and forth to therapy for the first few days. Eventually he was able to use a regular chair and more and more, others were able to get him into it without calling for Jamie. Damn.

He'd really liked it when he had an excuse to spend time with Grant. They had become good friends. Grant had been flabbergasted when Jamie had come in one day with a large shopping bag.

"What in the world is that?" Grant had asked, his brows raising.

"Well, like I said, usually there are lots of visitors for patients and they bring in what's needed. The therapists prefer for you to wear shorts and T-shirts for therapy. That wasn't possible with the way you were trussed up, but now you need clothes, man. I don't know what happened to all your stuff from before, but this is just the basics. Nothing special, don't get all freaked out."

"I'm not. Hey, thanks. I'll pay you back. What's in there?" Grant looked eager.

Jamie set the bag in the chair by Grant's bed and reached in for the three pairs of sweats he'd bought. He figured two of them could be cut off into shorts and the other could be kept for when Grant could get them on over the cast on his ankle. There were a couple of shirts and several pairs of boxers. He hadn't known what Grant preferred, but with the ankle cast, the knee brace and the dressing on his torn groin muscle, right now boxers made sense. The last thing he brought out of the bag was a pair of brown moccasins. Grant's eyes lit up.

"Oh, thanks so much. For all of it, but especially for those. I owe you, big time. I won't forget." Grant looked up at Jamie. "You're a really thoughtful person, aren't you? You think about people and go out of your way to do things for them. I wish I was like that." His voice took on a little bit of wistfulness.

"Hey, it's not a big deal," Jamie said, meaning it. "I just figured you needed these things and I was going by to get dog food anyway, so I fixed you up."

Grant's eyes went wide. "You have a dog? What kind? A big dog? What's its name?"

"Whoa, I've never seen you so interested in *any*thing," Jamie said, smiling. "You into dogs? Do you have one—oh my God, if you do, who's taking care of it?" It suddenly hit Jamie that if Grant lived alone but had a dog, he would be frantic about it.

The saddest look came over Grant's face. He closed his eyes for a minute and didn't say anything. He turned his head away, obviously not wanting Jamie to see his face.

"Oh, man. Tell me you were by yourself in that car. Tell me…Grant, you can tell me."

"He's gone. I do remember them telling me that. Roger's gone," he said. There were tears in his voice as he told it. "I've had him for three years. Never thought one animal could mean so much, but we were buds, you know?" He finally looked up at Jamie, letting him see the tears in his eyes.

"I'm so sorry. Really," Jamie said, grabbing a tissue and handing it to Grant in a matter of fact fashion, like it was nothing to see tears on a grown man at the loss of his dog. Grant took it and used it, thanking Jamie again with his eyes.

"Tell me about Roger," Jamie urged, quietly, as he moved the bag and sat on the chair.

"I don't know if I can. It's still a little raw," Grant started then took a deep shuddering breath and did it anyway. He wiped his arm across his eyes and looked over at Jamie and told his story. "Roger was a gift from my team my first year as a coach. We went all the way to state and were on cloud nine. The guys were always hassling me 'cause...well, 'cause I was always alone. Why does that bother everybody so much? It's just how my life's been." Grant looked bewildered, but kept on. "Anyway, they got me this golden retriever pup, and I could tell by the size of his paws he was gonna be huge. He was a horse. Roger was my best friend. We did everything together. So, see, I wasn't really alone. I just couldn't tell you that I'd killed my only companion." Grant closed his eyes on the pain again.

"Shit. You need to quit thinking like that, Grant," Jamie said, firmly. "You know that's not true. You weren't driving drunk, you weren't in the wrong lane, going too fast, or asleep at the wheel. Come on," he cajoled, wanting Grant to admit that Roger's death was not his fault.

"I know here," Grant pointed to his head but then touched his chest over his heart, "but I don't believe it here. If I'd left him home, he'd still be alive, and..."

Jamie broke in. "And he'd be what? Alone in your house or apartment? I don't know how you live, but you don't seem to have people to come in and take care of him. Would you be worried about him starving to death? He died a happy dog, Grant. I know that sounds stupid, but you know it's true. He was with his master, whom he loved. You said it yourself. You all were best friends." Jamie knew he was reaching.

There were probably people who could have gone in and cared for Roger, but right now, he was trying to cheer up Grant. "He would have missed you and not known what to do without you all this time. Now I'm not sayin' it was a good thing, but well, I just need you to focus on yourself. Get better."

"Wow. You just put it out there, don't you? You're right," Grant said. "I'll miss him, but I'll get over it."

"Nah, now, you're not getting it. You take your time and grieve for him. I totally understand. Lord knows what I'd do without Whistlebritches. I'd go through a major meltdown."

Grant's brows rise, and his eyes go wide at his dog's name. Most people did.

Jamie finished, before Grant could ask about it. "I just want you to get over thinking it was your fault."

"Okay. I get it. I'll work on it," Grant said, finally summoning a smile and coming with the expected, "Whistlebritches?"

"Well, I call him Brit, but when he was little he'd grab my britches legs and tug and tug, but if I whistled real loud, he'd drop them and sit right in front of me. So I forgot the name I'd originally called him, Thunder, and he became Whistlebritches. I remember the father of one of my friends calling him that when we were in grade school. I always thought it was funny."

"I can just hear you yelling for him to come in for dinner." Grant laughed at him.

"Here, Brit, come on, boy," Jamie teased back.

"Ah, yeah. I forgot. Brit. Good save. Oh, and…Thunder?" Grant asked about Brit's original name.

"Dude, even as a little puppy, that dog had the loudest farts you've ever heard. Thunder made sense, believe me."

Grant laughed aloud at Jamie's face as he told the story. Jamie felt good that he'd made Grant relax a little and smile.

"Hey, I gotta head out. I saved you for last, but I need to get things finished and go hit the books before bed. I'll see you tomorrow." Jamie got up and put Grant's clothes in the closet space.

"Hey?" Grant said and waited for Jamie to turn back to him.

"Yeah?" Jamie asked, turning.

"Thanks. I look forward to seeing you tomorrow," Grant said while looking right into Jamie's eyes.

Wow.

Jamie was almost tongue-tied. "Uh, me, too." He gave a quick wave and went out.

He turned out of Grant's room and stopped a second to lean back against the wall. Whew. He thought he might be having a hot flash. Was Grant coming on to him? God, he hoped so. Down boy, he thought.

Jamie dreamed about Grant that night. He woke about four-thirty in the morning with a hard-on and Grant's name on his lips. The good thing was it was one of those dreams he could remember. So, as his hand had moved up and down his stiff cock, he let his mind wander back over what had occurred in his dream.

Grant was whole again, tall, and walking. The two of them had been on Jamie's back porch, after cooking out together. They shared a lounger and laughed as it creaked and groaned at the doubled weight. Laughter had soon turned into groans and sighs as they discovered ways to turn each other on. Jamie had sucked on one of Grant's nipples while his hand slid into Grant's jeans. Grant was just as busy with one hand on the back of Jamie's neck and the other clasping his behind. Grant had just moved his hand up and was sliding it down inside the back of Jamie's jeans when Jamie had woken, panting.

He lay there thinking about Grant's body and his luscious lips and before long his hand was covered with hot cum, and he was breathing like he'd raced for the gold. He cleaned up and turned over, finally getting back to sleep with visions of Grant fuelling more night time fantasies.

Hell, he didn't even know if the man was gay, and he was having sex dreams about him. Not knowing Grant's persuasion, he decided to let Grant set the pace in their friendship. If he wanted more, Jamie was so there. If not, well, he could always use another friend.

When Jamie got up the next day, he called a friend and asked a favour of him. He showed up at work with a bounce in his step. He checked the day's schedule for his patients then called his friend again. Grant would be in his room after his therapy session at one-thirty with free time until about four. He hoped his plan would work well and not fall flat.

Jamie checked in with each patient and the day flew by. Miss Wilhemina felt better, and they teased each other playfully. He said good-bye to Mr. Jenson, who had progressed very well and was going home. After taking Grant down to therapy, he spent a couple of minutes watching his session. Grant worked hard and got along well with the therapist. Jamie could tell the movements caused him a lot of pain, but he didn't complain.

When he returned later to pick him up, Grant was pale and sweating.

"Dude, did you overdo a little today? You look wiped out," Jamie said, knowing that doing too much was as bad as not doing enough.

"Nah, I'll be fine. I'm just tired. I didn't sleep too well last night, and I had another session this morning before you got here. I'll rest a little now."

Jamie rolled him back to his room and helped him into the bathroom. He braced Grant as he stood on his good leg and looked the other way as he used the bathroom. Jamie knew men wanted to do this for themselves as soon as it was physically possible. It just seemed like this one thing made them feel like they were on the road to recovery.

Soon, he settled Grant back into the bed. He went and got a cloth and ran warm water in the sink. He gave Grant a quick wash off. There wasn't time right now for a bath, but he smoothed the cloth over Grant's face, neck, arms and legs then flipped up the sheet.

"Why don't you nap a few minutes there, tough guy?" Jamie said. *Why don't I just crawl right up in there with you?*

"Thanks, Jamie." Grant eyes closed as Jamie stepped out.

He got his mind back on business and went to meet his friend at the front door. His friend was no stranger to this facility. Brandon had been coming here for the last year and a half with different working dogs. He was part of the program that brought the dogs in as encouragement and support for the patients.

When the dogs were here, they wore a vest-like thing that meant they were not to be approached by staff and petted as usual. They were here for the patients, and they'd been trained for just this work. Today, Brandon had gone by and picked up Jamie's dog, Whistlebritches, who had finished the training several months before. Brit was a Golden Labrador, very big, strong, and healthy.

Jamie and Brandon took Brit around the different halls and went to room after room to visit the patients who were known to respond well to the animals. Miss Wilhemina especially loved Brit. She'd seen him twice now, and she squealed and clapped her hands when she saw them at the door, asking permission to come in.

"Oh, Jamie, you've brought Brit to see me. Come here, boy. Oh, how I love him. I miss being around animals." She'd lived on a farm for most of her life and missed being outside, but she missed the animals most. He gave the command to Brit who went to the side of Miss Wilhemina's bed and lay his head on it for her to pet his head.

"Can I get up in the chair, Jamie? I want to be able to reach him better," she pleaded. There wasn't not a person alive who could have turned her down.

They made the switch, and she bent from the waist and hugged Brit, who stood still and took it with just a wag of his tail. She pulled back, looked into Brit's eyes and told him quietly what a wonderful dog he was and how he was doing a good thing. He licked her hand, and she giggled like a little girl.

It had been almost an hour since Grant had returned to his room so Jamie figured he'd had a good nap. He'd saved him for last and told Brandon that he'd like to take this one by himself if it was all right. Brandon went to get a cold drink and said he'd be in the lounge when Jamie was ready for him to take Brit home.

Jamie knocked on Grant's partially open door and when he got a response he leaned in and said, "I've got someone for you to meet. May we come in?"

"Uh, sure. Come on." Grant pushed a button and the head of his bed came up further. His eyes widened and he smiled widely when he saw the dog next to Jamie.

Jamie and Brit went to the left side of the bed then Jamie touched the dog, giving him the signal to shake hands. Brit raised his paw to the bed and waited for Grant to shake it. Grant reached out and shook the big paw.

"Who's this?" he asked, moving his hand to rub the top of Brit's head.

"Grant, this is Brit, my best bud. Brit, this is my new friend, Grant. Up, Brit," Jamie commanded, telling Brit he could put both paws and his head up to reach Grant.

When he did, Grant put both arms around Brit's neck and put his face against Brit's neck. Brit took it like he was trained to do. He stood still and let Grant love on him. Grant pulled back, and Jamie saw him rub his arm across his eyes.

Jamie touched Brit and pulled him down to stand beside the bed.

"Is it all right? Do you want us to leave? Not a good idea? I was hoping…"

"No, don't go. I just…please stay. Can you help me sit on the side of the bed a minute?" Grant asked.

"Sure. Easy now." He helped Grant ease up to a sitting position.

"Will he come over here?" Grant asked, looking up at Jamie and gesturing to Brit.

"Sure. Brit, go to Grant. Relax, Brit." When he said that, Brit gave a happy bark, put his paws up on the bed on Grant's left side and nuzzled into him. He reached up and licked Grant's face and whined when Grant laughed and hugged him again.

Jamie's heart thudded hard against his chest as he relaxed. He'd done a good thing. There had been that chance that Grant would hate seeing Brit after losing Roger. But, he obviously loved dogs and was happy to respond to Brit.

Grant looked up at Jamie and reached out one hand to him. Jamie took his hand and squeezed, accepting the thank you from Grant.

Jamie admitted quietly, "I was a little afraid, but I know Brit and I'm beginning to know you. You need some love in your life, dude. You can get it from Brit here for now."

"I'm beginning to think I need more than just Brit," Grant admitted, never taking his hand off the dog or his eyes off Jamie.

"Oh, man. That sounds…uh…promising. I hope. I think. I'm afraid to hope you mean what I hope you mean." Jamie had turned into a blithering idiot. "Now that was just eloquent, wasn't it? I'm not usually so swave and deboner," he teased, making a play on the words suave and debonair.

Grant laughed with him and continued rubbing Brit's head. Brit now rested his head on Grant's thigh, right about where Jamie wanted to rest *his* head. Bang. Hard-on. He turned a little and sat down in the chair by the bed. He figured they had maybe another five minutes or so for Grant to soak up the love Brit gave so freely. Jamie found himself wishing Grant would say more about what he needed.

"Tell me about Brit. He's yours, but did you get him from the program?" Grant asked then patted the bed and laughed as the huge dog jumped right up beside him and lay with his head back on Grant's thigh. Now Grant could rub his hand all down Brit's back and neck as well as his head. They were both in a mutual form of heaven, and Jamie had to accept Grant's change of subject. Grant obviously wasn't comfortable with what Jamie hoped were the beginnings of feelings for *him.*

"No, I've had Brit since he was just little. After I started working here and saw the program my friend Brandon had going, I knew I wanted to see if Brit would work out. Seems he's perfect for it. He's big so he can take the rough handling he gets sometimes when someone gets overzealous." He reached over and added his hand to Grant's on Brit's head. Their hands touched, neither pulled away. "He's also a gentle giant. You saw how still he stood until I released him. He's very smart. He knows how to stay away from injured areas, how to ease up to people, and how to give them just what they want. He seems to be able to read people." Jamie sat back and just watched his dog and his friend. "And, by the way, this is the first time he's been up on a bed with a patient. It seems you're special to him, too." He added the last and watched to see how Grant took it.

Grant smiled.

God, the man's mouth!

Chapter Three

Grant had begun to watch the door and sighed when he saw Jamie heading in. He realised that he'd waited for him and relaxed when he arrived. He'd done a lot of soul searching lately. The day was coming when he would have to talk with Jamie about where the two of them were headed. He dreaded that, since he didn't know what he would say. Jamie seemed to have it all together and know what he wanted. He was comfortable with himself. Grant, on the other hand, wasn't sure of himself at all. He just knew he was getting closer and closer to Jamie. He even admitted to himself that he was interested in a sexual way, something he'd never been able to admit before.

Grant had dated a little through the years but never seriously. He'd never been that interested in women. He'd dated for appearance sake since he had to be seen as 'normal', working with the teams as he did. He had never been able to admit to an interest in men, though. He knew, deep down, that he was. But he had always felt it was so wrong, and he couldn't bring himself to own it. He'd been taught by foster parents that it was an abomination. Later, he'd been around others who had mocked it. *It? Being gay.* There, he said it, silently, to himself. *Gay. I'm gay. Am I gay? I've gotta be. Don't I? God, I'm so confused.*

Then Jamie walked in.

* * * *

Jamie was good, really good. No one at work could tell that things had changed for him. He worked like he usually did. He took special care of his LOLs, joked with the staff and helped out where he was needed. Nope. No one seemed to be aware that he was really just living for the times when he got to see Grant. He couldn't wait to get to work. He made sure his breaks coincided with Grant's, the time between therapy sessions.

They neither one had said anything about…anything, but they were enjoying the time they spent together. They talked and found they liked a lot of the same things. Grant was grateful for Jamie's help where with others he resented having to ask for assistance with things.

"Boy, you look depressed," Jamie said as he stepped into Grant's room. "Therapy not going well? I thought you did great yesterday. What's with the long face?" He walked over to the bed.

Grant sat up straighter now, the pain having eased in his hip and his groin. He looked a little flushed. "Just thinking."

Jamie reached out to touch Grant's forehead, thinking he might have a fever.

"You look hot, man. You feeling okay?" It concerned him that Grant was acting weird, like he was worried or scared about something. "Anything I can do to help?"

"I'm doing some soul searching today, and I think I need to talk to someone."

Grant seemed embarrassed to admit that.

"Someone other than me, I take it," Jamie said, catching on, finally, to the fact that it was something about him that bothered Grant.

"Well, no. Yeah. Hell, Jamie, I'm so mixed up. I don't know what I need."

"Have I made you uncomfortable? Is it something about me? I don't want there to be a problem with us, man. I'll stay out of here."

"No!"

Okay.

"Sorry, I didn't mean to snap at you," Grant said, rubbing his hand over his face. "No, I don't want you to stay away. It's not a problem with you, it's me. I wish I knew how to talk about this. I'm...I need to figure out stuff."

"Grant, do you need me to go or stay, talk or shut up? I don't want to add to your problem, ya know?" Jamie felt compassion for Grant. He wondered if he was worried about where the two of them were going in their relationship, if they even had one. Jamie would love to think so, but he wasn't sure about Grant.

"What's the weather like out there? Is there a chance we can go out to the courtyard after my session this afternoon? I'd like to talk to you." Grant looked like he was gearing up for something momentous. "I need to talk to you about...uh...I just need to know some things so I'll know how to think."

"Sure. It's a nice day, and I'll try to be sure I have time after your session to be there with you. Okay, now?" Jamie was worried thinking that Grant would tell him they were getting too close and he wanted Jamie to ease off and not spend so much time with him.

"Yeah, that'd be great. Thanks." Grant smiled, a little hesitantly.

When Jamie left the room he was almost shaking. He hoped Grant wasn't going to tell him to leave him alone. He'd thought they were really connecting and liked each other, equally. Maybe it was all on his side. God, he'd hate that.

He spent the time between seeing Grant and...seeing Grant again, doing all the things he was used to doing. Thank heaven, he was able to do it without thinking. He was just as flirty with the LOLs and helped them with myriad problems, he lifted a new patient who weighed over three hundred pounds, and he spent some time talking with Jackie about her kids and what was going on with them.

He was busy when it was time for Grant to go to therapy, so someone else took him down, but he worked it out so he had a break due when it was time to pick up Grant after his session. He grabbed a couple snacks and boxes of juice and dropped them into Grant's lap when he picked him up.

"Great. I'm starving." Grant smiled up at Jamie as he wheeled him out the door of the gym and headed the other way today. They were going on an outing, so to speak. They'd be within sight of most of the rooms as the courtyard was in the centre of the complex and all the inside rooms looked out on it. There was no such thing as privacy, but they would be able to speak freely.

Jamie looked down at the top of Grant's head as he pushed his chair. Grant was a handsome man. He had a full head of silky dark hair. It needed a cut, he thought, as he made himself quit thinking about the appeal of the man. The combination of nearly black hair and light blue eyes was pretty devastating to Jamie. He was so infatuated, he could fall hard with the least little bit of encouragement.

Jamie rolled Grant over to a picnic table and set the locks on his chair, then he sat on the bench close to Grant's chair so whatever Grant wanted to say would not be broadcast to anyone who might come near. Right now, they had the whole courtyard to themselves.

Jamie reached for the snacks in Grant's lap, thinking to divvy them between them, but ended up grabbing Grant's hand. He went to snatch back his hand in case Grant was uncomfortable, but Grant held on for a minute, giving him a squeeze. Jamie's heart thudded, and he sucked in a big drink of air. He slowly eased out of Grant's grip and managed not to look around like he'd done something wrong.

Grant handed a pack of crackers and a box of juice to Jamie then opened his own without saying a word. The silence stretched, then…

"How long have you known you were gay?" Grant asked, bluntly.

Not being one to beat around the bush, either, Jamie answered, "A long time."

"Do you...uh...date a lot? Know a lot of guys? You said you went out a lot," Grant said, squinting a little in the sun.

"No. None. I mean, I don't date...a lot. I haven't been on a real date in more than two years. I've been busy, and there hasn't been anyone I was interested in. I have a lot of friends who are just that, friends. We hang out when we have time. A bunch of us who don't have anyone but don't want to be alone all the time go out occasionally. That clear as mud? I'm unattached right now."

"Me, too. I mean...Jamie, I've never even admitted to myself I was gay. I knew it, I guess. I just couldn't put the name to it. There are reasons why I've lived in denial all these years. My past, my upbringing, the foster parents and the crowd I was forced to be around. I was so deeply in the closet I was never able to come out. And I guess I never met anyone who made me want to admit to myself or others that I'm gay. I'm queer. I'm still lost. I don't know what to do now."

"You don't have to *do* anything. Want to tell me what brought on this sudden need to verbalise what you've been hiding from in the past?" Jamie knew what he hoped the answer was going to be. Why would Grant tell him this if it didn't have something to do with him? Maybe he was just looking for advice or guidance from someone who knew the score, so to speak.

"You have to know, it's because of you," Grant said. He looked at Jamie, and a slow smile touched his mouth. "I've been happy to just be damn near asexual for years. I haven't been one or the other. I've not been interested in women and afraid to be interested in men so I've been a damn eunuch."

Jamie winced. "I know what you're saying. I mean, I'm no virgin, as I suppose you're saying you are, but it's been so long since I've been with anyone I might need a refresher course." He laughed a little, but it was true. He'd begun to think he had a low libido since he seemed to be all right without anyone in his life. Grant's appearance in his life had changed that thinking. He'd come back to full life in that area. He wanted the man with a ferocious need that he had to keep in check with a strong will.

"My life is so screwed up right now. I don't know what I'm going to do when I get out of here. They've replaced me at the school where I was working, and I totally understand. I'm kind of in limbo."

"Do you know if they're suggesting you continue with therapy after they release you?"

"Yeah, how'd you know? They talked about it yesterday. They said I should come in for about a month to two months after I'm released. I guess I can find a place in Crandall or nearby, but I'm not sure." Grant was silent a few minutes, thinking about what he might be able to arrange.

"I'm going to go way out on a limb here and do something really strange," Jamie said, feeling like a gumball machine. The idea came into his head and just rolled right off his tongue.

"I've got an extra bedroom you could use. I come in almost every day. I have friends who could shuttle you back and forth on the times when I couldn't." Jamie hadn't even thought it all out before he rattled off the invitation. It just made sense to him.

Grant looked shocked. "Jamie, you can't do that. You can't just open your home to someone you've only known a few weeks."

"Yeah, actually I can. It's not like I don't know you. I do, and I like you. I don't think we'd have any trouble getting along. I don't want you to think I'm suggesting any kind of relationship other than roommates, but you're kind of stuck needing a place to stay near the facility, and I have the room. We know we get along. It makes sense."

"I'd have to think about it. It sounds good. I'm not usually one for spur of the moment decisions, but I was wondering what I was going to do for therapy. I'm not finishing out the year at school, so my time is my own. I can do whatever I want to. It sounds great, but are you sure you want to do that? I'm not exactly low maintenance." Grant pointed to his casts.

"That's another reason it would be a good idea. You won't be on your own. I can help if you need it. By the time, they release you, you'll almost be independent, but you might need help, and I'm certainly capable, yeah?" Jamie smiled at him, his heart happy, thinking he might be getting a roomie.

Grant laughed a little. "You're serious. You really want to do this."

"I really do," Jamie said then got serious and added, "And as far as the other thing goes, don't worry. I'm not gonna jump your bones. I have friends who'll be over now and then. You might find you like one of them and want to explore your new feelings..."

"No."

"Sorry?" Jamie looked up, quickly at the short answer.

"No, I'm not interested in meeting one of your friends in the hopes of getting together with him. The only reason I'm admitting to these feelings at all is because of you. I'm interested in *you*, Jamie, you."

Yes!

"Do I have a shit-eatin' grin on my face? I know I do." He felt the smile splitting his face from ear to ear. "I'm way past just interested in you, but I would never push you into anything. I want you to know that."

"I'm not worried. We'll find our way together. Just knowing the feeling is mutual is nice, even if I don't know how to act on it. I'm excited just thinking about spending time with you, though. Is that okay to say?"

"God, yes. It's all I can do not to grab you and kiss you right here," Jamie admitted.

Neither heard anyone approaching, but both were stunned when they heard Donnie behind them.

"Oh, a picnic. How sweet. Is this part of your job, Jamie-boy? I never knew that." Donnie's voice was full of spite and malice. Jamie wouldn't give him the satisfaction of turning to face him.

"I'm on my break, and Grant just finished therapy. I thought some sun would be good for him," Jamie answered, though he hated explaining himself to Donnie. "I brought Miss Wilhemina out here earlier after her therapy. So, yeah, it's part of my job. What's your problem, Donnie?"

Jamie wasn't going to take any more shit from Donnie. He'd had it.

"I believe I heard them paging you as I came out the door. You run on inside, and I'll push Grant back to his room." Donnie suggested.

"No way in hell. I'll take him back and go see where I'm needed." Donnie didn't work at the facility and there was no way that Jamie would turn Grant over to him. He could tell Grant was with him on that from the relieved look on his face.

"Whatsa matter, Jamie? Afraid to leave me alone with your boyfriend?"

"What are you yapping about, Donnie?" Jamie got chills thinking Donnie might have heard what they were talking about. Sneak. Bastard. "Excuse me. I'm taking Grant back to his room and getting back to work. My break is over in a few minutes, anyway." Jamie got behind Grant, unlocked his chair and turned to head back inside.

Donnie made the mistake of grabbing his arm, strongly enough to jerk the chair.

"Let go of my arm, right now, Donnie. You really don't want to go there," Jamie snarled, the menace in his voice real. No one grabbed him, especially when he was dealing with a patient. Double that 'especially' when it was a patient he had strong feelings for.

"Ooooh, tough guy. Turns me on. How about you, Grant? You like Jamie rough like that?" Donnie let go of Jamie and moved around in front of Grant so he was walking backwards on the sidewalk, talking down to Grant.

"Jamie, is there somewhere I can report harassment? I'm sure there's some kind of protocol involved. It can't be the first time this man has irritated the hell out of someone."

Well, damn. Grant had balls to spare.

"I can get the forms for you from the office. I'll see that you're not bothered again. I'm sorry about this,

Grant." Jamie talked to Grant as if Donnie wasn't right there listening.

"Try it, Gimpy. Just try turning me in and see how long your sweetie will last here." Donnie stopped and Jamie had to pull back so he didn't ram Grant's chair into him. Not a bad idea, really, but not prudent.

"Move, Donnie. I've got work to do. I'll take Grant to his room then maybe you and I can go to the office together. Is your father in this afternoon? I believe we should talk to him together." Jamie looked right at Donnie to let him know he was not afraid of him. "I'll take my chances with him believing me. Let's go."

Jamie didn't wait. He started moving the chair, and Donnie had no choice but to turn and skedaddle. Jamie hurried Grant to his room, got him settled and paused only when Grant said his name as he was leaving the room.

"Jamie?"

"Yeah?" Jamie turned back to Grant for a moment.

"Be careful. I think there's something really off about that man. He's dangerous." Grant was worried, Jamie could tell. Hell, he was worried himself.

He'd been lulled into a false sense of security the last few days with Donnie not showing himself. Now he was back and up to worse tricks than before.

"I will. But I'm not going to have him terrorising you or me. I'm tired of him dogging me and…well, it's time to put a stop to it one way or another."

He stopped at the nurse's desk to find that no one had paged him. Hmph. Liar. Okay. He headed to Bob's office and saw that the door was closed. He asked Marie, the secretary, if Bob was busy. She looked nervous.

"He's in there, but Donnie's in there with him, and he's been yelling. I'm not trying to cause problems, but your name came up a couple of times."

"I'm going in."

Jamie went around her desk, knocked quickly on the door then opened it and stepped in without waiting for an invitation.

Bob Wilkins looked at him as he came in and his shoulders slumped. He raked his hand through his hair and sat back down in his chair.

"Jamie. I'm...uh...glad you came by. I need to clear something up. Donnie here claims..."

"Sir, may I say something first? Please." Jamie was going to lay it on the line, straight out, and see what Bob had to say.

Bob looked at him for a moment and then said, "Jamie, I've always liked you. I consider you an asset to this facility. I figure I owe you that much, though I'm disturbed by what Donnie has been saying."

"I understand. I'm a little upset by what Donnie has been saying myself. I'm going to tell you the straight out truth." Jamie took a deep breath and started his speech without ever looking at Donnie, who now stood fuming by the window.

"I love my job here. I'm good at it, am studying to be a physical therapist and would love to work here when that happens. I've never had a problem in any area except one. About six months after I started working here, Donnie started hassling me. It was in small ways at first, so I ignored it. He made remarks that were pointed to the fact he thought he knew something about me that was in some way bad. He alluded to the possibility of my losing my job if he went to you with his knowledge. There've been numerous occasions where he's been what I consider inappropriate in his remarks to me. Since he's your son, I've ignored it.

"Bob, I'll say it straight out," Jamie said, maybe willing to do so since he'd just been talking with Grant. "I'm gay. I don't know if that makes any difference to you or not. I don't think anyone here even knows it, but Donnie has always suspected. I don't know how, but he has held it over my head for the last time." He looked right at Bob the whole time he talked, trying to gauge if this knowledge made a difference to him. "I've not had a relationship with anyone in the last two years, at all. I have worked and gone to class and studied. That's it. No lie. So, I don't know what he thinks he has on me, but there's no basis for it.

"Recently a new patient came in, and Donnie has implied more than once that there was something going on between me and this patient. He accosted me the first day this patient was here and accused me of having the hots for him. I didn't even know the man." Jamie ran his hands through his hair, frustrated at having to bring all this up at all. "I'm tired of it. Donnie even went so far as to go to this patient's room and tell him that he, Donnie, and I, were a couple. That was a definite lie.

"I will admit to you that I have developed a friendship with this patient and have just today offered him my spare room while he continues his therapy here at the facility." He figured he might as well admit it to Bob now, so there was no problem later if there was something about the situation that

Bob couldn't handle. He needed to know now. "If Donnie is right, and he has the power to get me fired because I don't have feelings for him and won't see him away from here, then let me know now. I'll start looking for another job. But I won't be hassled and threatened anymore." He was getting upset, but tried to keep his voice even. "Besides that, he lied to me today and told me I'd been paged and that he would push this patient back to his room. Donnie does not work here. I wasn't about to let him near a patient after the things he'd said. Oh, and I checked. I had not been paged. That's it. The ball's in your court. That's the honest truth."

Jamie felt as if he needed to drag in great gulps of air. He wasn't sure he'd breathed the whole time. He'd just spoken in a steady voice, no inflection, no yelling. He hadn't even looked at Donnie. He knew that once during the long talking he'd done, Donnie had started to say something, but Bob had held up his hand and stopped him.

Now Bob took both hands and rubbed them over his face. There was silence for a few minutes. Jamie heard a clock ticking on the wall and thought it was the sound of his future ticking away. He glanced at Donnie for a split second and saw that he stood with his fists drawn and shaking.

"Well. Uh, I'm at a loss here. Two different stories. What to do. What to do." Bob sat for another few seconds then turned to his son and said, "Sit down, Donnie."

"Dad, come on, I..."

"Sit *down*, Donnie. I've wondered why you've spent so much time here recently. I know you're not interested in the work. I've heard some of your comments about the people here, and they are…lacking in respect, shall we say?" He held up his hand again to stop Donnie from interrupting. "I'm inclined to believe Jamie's version of things. What do you have to say, young man?" Donnie had thrown himself into his chair. Jamie was shocked to see tears in his eyes, running down his face.

"Dad, he's lyin'. He's been coming on to me for the longest time. You can ask anybody. He's a fag. I'm…"

Bob looked over at Jamie when he gasped at this lie and the slur that followed.

"Sir, as I said, I don't think anyone here even knows I'm gay. It has never come up. So no one will tell you I've ever come on to anybody, especially Donnie. I'm sorry if this is upsetting for you, but your son is lying, and I'd appreciate it if, well, if you decide to keep me on here, that none of this comes out. I don't want people uncomfortable, and I know some might be. To me, it should be a nonissue, but I know that's not possible with some people."

"I know what you mean. Jamie, I don't care a fig about your sexual preference. It's never interfered with your work, and I don't expect it to in the future. I certainly have no intention of firing you, and it's not because you would have good grounds for a helluva lawsuit. You go on and finish your work and let me handle Donnie. I think it's time my son and I had a talk. I'm sorry you were uncomfortable."

Jamie was in a state of shock. He'd hoped that Bob would be reasonable, but he was surprised it was so easy. Whew.

He stood to leave. As he did so, he glanced at Donnie and shivered at the cold hatred in his eyes. Oh, shit. Things might be settled with Bob, but not with Donnie. Jamie felt sure he would hear more from Donnie. He knew he'd better watch his back. He hoped that Grant would be safe here, too. Damn, he really hated this situation.

He knew he probably shouldn't, but he went straight to Grant's room and closed the door firmly. Grant looked at him and held out his hand.

"Tell me. How bad was it?" His hand was still out, waiting for Jamie to take it. Jamie didn't hesitate. He needed to be touched right now. He shook from leftover emotion, fear and anxiety about Donnie's malice and the form it would take now.

Grant moved his thumb back and forth over Jamie's knuckles as he listened to the story of how the meeting went. He sucked in his breath when Jamie told him about Donnie's threatening look.

"I know it's not over, Grant. He'll come after me, and now it'll be worse."

"We'll deal with whatever, Jamie," Grant said. He pulled Jamie's hand to his mouth and planted a quick kiss on it then looked so surprised at himself that Jamie had to laugh.

"I'm gonna guess this is the first time you've ever kissed a man." He smiled down at Grant who blushed.

"Okay, make fun. I can take it." Grant laughed with him.

"Oh, no, not making fun. I love it, but I gotta get back to work. Later."

Just a kiss on the hand from Grant had him higher than full out sex with some men in the past.

* * * *

The next few days passed without incident. Jamie went to class, studied, went to work, and spent as much time with Grant as he could. Grant was making great progress. His attitude was greatly improved, it seemed, and it had a positive effect on his therapy sessions.

There were a few opportunities for more touching between the two of them. Nothing major, but they were getting closer, more comfortable with each other. The trips to the courtyard after Grant's afternoon therapy sessions continued. They enjoyed the time together to talk and enjoy the sunshine.

Jamie brought Brit in a couple more times, and Grant was obviously thrilled to see him. Brit formed an attachment to Grant, also. Jamie always let him relax and as soon as the command was given, he was up on the bed with Grant, much to Grant's delight.

He even brought by Miss Wilhemina to meet Grant, and the three of them had a good time talking and laughing. They talked about Brit and what a great dog he was. Miss Wilhemina told Grant about growing up on a farm and working with the animals and how she'd loved it. She admitted she had a crush on Jamie, and Jamie blushed when Grant leaned over and whispered into her ear, making her smile and look up at Jamie with bright eyes.

Jamie thought about taking Grant out on an outing. Grant had reached the stage where he could go out for a couple of hours with the right kind of help, so Jamie took it upon himself to ask the therapists and Grant's doctor if he was ready for the trip, and they agreed he was. They expressed surprise that Grant had someone to take him out as no one had appeared to visit him yet. Jamie admitted he was going to do it himself. He was glad no one made any comments about it.

He planned on surprising Grant with the idea after his session that afternoon. He hoped Grant would be up for the plan. He hadn't decided on where to take him, though it would probably be best to just take him to his house, let him play with Brit a little then bring him back. Grant would get to see the place and get an idea of what it would be like to live there with Jamie.

He had snacks with him when he picked up Grant and smiled as he rolled him out the door to the courtyard. Grant was doing a little more each day with his arms. He took over a little of the pushing of the chair, though Jamie noticed him wincing as it pulled on his shoulder. Jamie let him do a little but wouldn't let him push himself to the point of pain.

When they were settled at the picnic table, Grant asked, "What are you grinning at? You seem awfully happy. What's up?"

"How would you like to come to my house for a couple of hours on Saturday?" Jamie watched Grant's expression.

"Really? I can leave? That sounds great! How'd you work it?" Grant's eyes lit up, a smile growing to spread wide across white teeth. The man looked happy, and Jamie beamed back at him.

"It's usually part of the recovery process, but most people have family members who come to take them out for a few hours." Jamie smiled at him. "You're stuck with me."

"Thank God," Grant said.

"So, you'll come to the house with me for a couple hours? You can see the place and get a feel for it. Brit will be ecstatic. He really likes you. Runs in the family," Jamie said, smiling into Grant's eyes.

"I'm glad."

They talked animatedly for a while about Saturday, then Jamie rolled Grant back to his room. When they got there Grant pointed to the door and asked if Jamie would close it. Looking, questioningly at him, Jamie did then turned back to find Grant right there behind him. He was almost pinned to the door.

Grant looked up at him and raised his hand, crooking his finger. "Will you come down here for a minute? I'd really...really like to kiss you. Or have you kiss me since I don't know that much about what I'm doing. I just think about it all the time and..."

He never got to finish. Jamie had thought about it nearly nonstop himself. Before Grant completed his request, Jamie granted it. He put both hands on the arms of Grant's chair and gasped when it started to roll. He reached down and locked it then planted his hands again. He leaned in and loved that Grant held his face right up to his, asking for it, wanting it.

While he wanted to take Grant's mouth hard and just eat it, he thought about Grant's lack of experience. He made himself take a deep breath before starting their first real kiss. He put his lips to Grant's forehead, smiling a little at Grant's grunt of surprise. He knew Grant had expected that hard kiss, but he suddenly felt...gentle...tender. He slid his lips down the side of

Grant's face, stopping to place sweet kisses on each eye, down his nose to his chin. He pressed a little harder and let his tongue come out to caress the tip of Grant's chin, then slid to the front of his ear and licked another spot.

He felt Grant quiver. He leaned further and took Grant's lobe into his mouth and sucked for a second. Before he left that area, he slid his tongue out and laved the area right behind Grant's ear. He took note of the fact that Grant shivered and gave a tiny gasp. Jamie was enjoying himself.

Grant made an impatient sound, and Jamie took pity on him, going for his lips. He took his time, though. He touched his tongue to Grant's top lip then the bottom. Grant opened to him, and he eagerly swept in. He pushed his tongue into Grant's mouth and was thrilled when Grant met it with his own.

It began sweetly and tenderly, but at Grant's eager response, Jamie took it a step further and began to thrust in and out of Grant's mouth. He heard Grant's laboured breath and finally eased back a little, but he didn't want to let go. He put his forehead to Grant's, and they looked into each other's eyes for a few seconds, both stunned by how much they were feeling.

"Wow," Grant said, reverently. Jamie felt the same way. He looked down and saw an impressive hard-on tenting Grant's sweats. No doubt his own was equally as large. Jamie got brave and took Grant's left hand and brought it to his erection, gasping as he felt Grant's hand move just a little before pulling back.

He looked into Grant's eyes to see if he was upset at his being forward, but Grant reached out and took

Jamie's hand and brought it to his lap, inviting the same swift caress. Jamie traced the length of Grant and gave him a loving pat before reaching up to caress the side of Grant's face. He dropped a quick kiss on his lips and reached down to unlock the chair.

"I've probably just broken about forty'leven rules," Jamie said, ruefully. He wasn't sorry though.

"Forty'leven? Is that a lot?" Grant asked, smiling, as he reached down to propel the chair backward so Jamie could move away from the closed door.

"Yeah, a whole lot. I heard my cousin say it and it just stuck," Jamie said, helping Grant get the chair over to the bed so he could get into it. Jamie's break was definitely over.

He got Grant settled and decided that they were both going to act as if it hadn't happened. Neither knew what to say. It was just so big, so important. Jamie would come see Grant, as usual, before he left for the night. Maybe they'd be able to address it then. He could tell that Grant wasn't upset, but he looked a little shell-shocked. Jamie thought he might need a little time to process things.

When Jamie managed to get back to Grant's room right before he left, he found that Grant was sound asleep. That sometimes happened. It was eleven, after all. He stood for a moment beside Grant's bed, before reaching to move the hair off his forehead in a gentle caress. Jamie's heart beat a little faster just from looking at Grant sleeping. Damn, he had it bad.

Chapter Four

Finally, Saturday arrived. Jamie couldn't believe how excited he was. He was off today and tomorrow. It wasn't often that he had both weekend days off. He'd study tomorrow and play with Brit, but today he had Grant on the brain. He cleaned the place thoroughly in the morning then went to the store and shopped for groceries. He thought maybe he'd offer Grant a snack while he was there. He bought the juice he knew Grant loved and picked out some fruit for the counter in the kitchen.

Brit was bouncing more than usual. He could probably tell something was up as Jamie's eagerness and anticipation was transferred to him. Jamie headed out to pick up Grant at about one-thirty. There wasn't a lot of therapy on Saturdays so Grant was free until suppertime, but Jamie would make sure that Grant didn't get too tired. This would take a lot out of Grant, whether he knew it or not. Jamie would take good care of him.

When he got to the rehab facility he was surprised to find Grant in the lobby, ready to go. It looked like Jamie wasn't the only one excited about the trip. He did all the necessary paperwork needed to take Grant out for a while and rolled him out to his car, an old reliable Taurus. He loved it, and it would be fine for Grant. He pushed the passenger seat way back and helped Grant ease into it with his casted ankle going in last. Grant sighed deeply as he settled in. Jamie folded the wheelchair and put it in the back.

He got into the driver's seat and looked over at Grant. "You feel like you've been sprung from prison?"

"A little," Grant laughed. "I know I couldn't wait for you to get here. Oh, hey, I saw Donnie while ago, right before you showed up."

"Shit! Did he do anything? Say anything to you?" Jamie's heart pounded. He'd been lulled into a false sense of security since they hadn't seen nor heard from the creep after Jamie's meeting with Bob.

"No. He gave me this glare, though. He's pure evil, man. He looked like he wanted to do something, but I was seated too close to the reception desk for him to follow through with anything."

"God, do you really think he would have done anything to you? That's scary, man. I don't get it. I don't know why he has this fixation on me. I really don't. In Bob's office, he made a big deal about me being a fag. Hello. Does Bob not know that Donnie leans that way? I mean, his actions seem to point to him wanting to be with me, not bash me for being gay. You know what I mean?" Jamie looked at Grant as he started the car.

"Yeah, the impression I got when he came to my room that time is that he was jealous of me, like I'd come to take you away from him. He was pretty clear on the fact that you were...his." Grant's expression was wary like he remembered the way Donnie had made him feel that day and since.

"I hate this," Jamie said, pulling out onto the road. "I'd rather just think about you and not worry about Devil Boy."

Grant snorted at Jamie's name for their nemesis. "I hear you. This is all so new to me. I'd like to think just about you and these new feelings."

"I'm so sorry I come with this baggage," Jamie said, meaning it.

"Don't even. I just feel like having a little tantrum and stomping my feet. Well, if I could stomp my feet." Grant smiled, ruefully. "For the first time in my life, something makes sense to me. You make sense to me. I want to explore this further." He stopped, glancing over at Jamie, seeming eager to get his reaction.

"I'm right there with you," Jamie said, smiling over at Grant.

"I don't want you to think I'm just using you to experiment with my sexuality. I would still be a total loser, a loner, if it wasn't for you. It's you I'm interested in, not just finally admitting to being gay. Knowing you has made me realise I want more. I want you, just you."

"Damn, dude, don't say things like that when I'm driving. I'd like to respond without worrying about staying on the road. You just sit there and be a good boy. I'll give you the quick tour of your new home for the near future."

Jamie pointed out a few things to Grant on their way to his house. The local park where he took Brit, the nearest mall, the theatre complex, the grocery. He turned into his subdivision, and Grant's eyes widened.

"This is nice. How can you afford something like this? Oh, now that was nosy. I'm sorry." Grant seemed appalled that he had asked something like that.

"No, it's okay. It was my parents'. They've been gone a couple of years now. It was left to me along with a good-sized life insurance policy. They died in a wreck. I can only be glad that they went together, because neither would have wanted to go on without the other. They were that close." He smiled as he thought of them, always together, so in love.

"That's cool, man—that they felt that way about each other, I mean. I'm sorry you lost them." Grant put his hand over on Jamie's arm for a second. Jamie looked over and winked at Grant.

"Thanks. Come on, let's get you inside, and I'll give you the tour then we can settle for a snack and some conversation without fear of interruption. How's that sound?" Jamie turned off the car and looked at Grant.

"Sounds good, let's do it." He unbuckled and waited for Jamie to get out and get his chair. He looked forward to the time he wouldn't need it. Right now, he couldn't even use crutches because of his shoulder and arm. He'd borrowed a ramp from one of the other techs who often had a sister visit him who was in a wheelchair, so getting into the house wouldn't be a problem.

Brit met them at the door, his tail wagging so hard his whole behind looked like a pendulum gone crazy. He barked a welcome to Grant.

"Back up, Brit. Let us in. You can love on Grant in a minute. Good boy," Jamie said, when Brit obeyed. Jamie pushed Grant in, closed the door and sighed.

"There, we've officially escaped. What do you want to do first?" Jamie moved around to look down at Grant.

"I'd like to see the place like you suggested then stop by the bathroom then come in here and get out of this chair and onto that wonderful-looking couch, so we can be on the same level for once. Then maybe...another kiss...or two?" He added the last with such hesitation that Jamie took pity on him and bent down, planting one on him right then.

He just dove in, pushed until Grant's mouth opened and thrust inside. No easy kiss, this. It seemed he wanted to inhale the man. He swept inside and delighted in the immediate response he got. Jamie held onto the chair arms again and kept on, not realising that he was forcing Grant's head backwards until he heard a moan. Having to ease up a little, he slowly gentled the kiss, an apology for getting out of control. He ended it but kept his head there, placing his cheek against Grant's, just breathing in for a moment.

"Sorry, but all it took was you saying the word, and I couldn't wait that long to kiss you," Jamie said, straightening up and looking down at a dazed Grant. Grant's lips looked soft and wet and delicious. Whew. He wanted more of them.

"No apology necessary, believe me. That was really the order I wanted to begin with but was afraid to ask."

"Okay, first order of business. Don't ever be afraid to ask for anything you want or to tell me about anything you don't like. There's a whole world of things we can do to make each other happy. You might like all of it or just some of it, but you have to tell me. Don't be shy, okay?" Jamie watched Grant blush but felt it had to be said.

"Yeah, I know about things. I've just never done any of them. I guess I've thought about them a lot, though, because the idea of doing some of the things I've heard and read about, with you, sends my heart into triple time."

Jamie laughed at that. "Great, I'm not alone in that, then. I've thought about you a lot and what I'd like to do with you. We'll go slow and not shock you back into celibacy, though."

"Not too slow. I'm new to all this but not unwilling. Now that I've finally admitted it to myself, I feel somehow free. I want to be with you. I know I'll be learning from you, but don't think I'm not eager. I want to make you feel good."

"Just being around you makes me feel good, and kissing you makes me hotter than a firecracker. God, if we ever make love, I'll probably lose it completely. It's what I want above all things, but that's for later. Let's go back to your agenda for now and see the place."

Brit had been so good. He'd sat and watched that whole exchange, but when it was obvious the two men were finally going to move, he came over for some lovin' from Grant.

"Hey, boy. How ya doin'?" Grant rubbed Brit's head and bent to put his face against Brit's neck. He appeared to be happy just being with Jamie's dog, the house, the freedom, and especially being with Jamie.

Jamie was a good host. He offered the bathroom trip first which Grant accepted. Grant was now able to get up from the chair and stand on his own so Jamie left him to it, though he left the door open so Grant could come out on his own. The tour followed, ending in the kitchen where Jamie got them some drinks and a plate of cheese, crackers and fruit. He carried it all into the living room and set it onto the table by the couch. He watched as Grant wheeled himself into the room, then he went to Grant and took over. Grant's arm would be hurting if he kept on using it like that.

Jamie moved the chair so it was close to the couch then went to the front of it and locked it. He put his arms gently under Grant's arms and lifted him. His plan had been to swing him around and ease him down to the couch, but once he had Grant standing right in front of him, he stopped and just looked at him. He made sure Grant was well-balanced, keeping one hand on him.

Jamie wanted Grant to feel he was on a somewhat equal footing as they stood and faced each other. They were about the same height, which would come in handy, Jamie thought. They'd fit together nicely.

"This is nice," Grant said, proving Jamie's instincts correct.

"I thought you might like it. You are one tall drink of water, aren't you?"

"Basketball player, remember? Yeah, I'm six foot four when I'm standing straight. This feels really good, but don't take that hand away. I'm not that steady."

"Don't worry. I'm not letting you go." Jamie meant that in more ways than one. "We're a good match. I'm six foot two. You'll top me by two."

"Yeah, but you've got the muscle mass to make you one really devastating example of male perfection," Grant said, chuckling.

"Damn, you're going to embarrass me," Jamie replied, actually blushing.

"I couldn't help it. I heard a couple of the nurses talking one day, and that's what they said about you."

"Good Lord, don't tell me which ones. I'll never be able to face them." Jamie laughed.

"I wanted to tell them I had plans for you, but I was still a little unsure of myself, and I'd never say anything anyway, but you get the idea. I just kept thinking how I'd like to agree with them. You're really sexy, you know that?" Grant tilted his head to one side, looking at Jamie from half-lowered lids.

"Okay, we better sit down or I'm gonna be the one who's not steady on his feet. God, you make me want," Jamie said, reaching to put his arms around Grant and pull him closer. Instead of helping him to sit, he took the opportunity to hug the man. Grant's arms came around him. His sore arm wrapped around Jamie's waist, but the left one went up around his neck.

They stood there for a few moments, relishing the joy of being able to hold one another in this position. Grant put his face down on Jamie's shoulder, and Jamie shivered as he felt Grant's breath on his neck. He tightened his arms, his hands moving on Grant's back. Grant moaned at the good feelings that clearly evoked. Jamie wanted to be able to make him feel this good all the time. The man needed a massage in a bad way. Jamie would be happy to oblige. He was sure Grant was tense and tired from all the therapy sessions, the pain and the worry.

"You're gonna get tired. Here, I'd better get you settled on the couch," Jamie finally said, pulling away before he wanted to let Grant go.

"Thanks, I liked that. It felt good." Still, Grant sighed in relief as Jamie helped him ease down onto the left corner of the couch, letting him rest his injured arm on the end of it. Jamie moved the chair out of the way and stood for a second looking at Grant.

"I'm going to be the good host here and give you a choice. See, I really want to spend some time kissing you. If you want that, too, let me know now. Let me know if you want your snack first or…"

He got no further as Grant leaned, grabbed his hand, and pulled him down to sit close beside him.

"Okay. Good to know." Jamie started, smiling.

"Shut up and kiss me," Grant said then laughed. "Didn't there used to be a song called that? Anyway, to borrow from the Nike commercials, just do it!"

Jamie leaned the little bit necessary to accomplish just that. They had time, plenty of time so he would make the most of it. He reached up and took Grant's face between his hands, holding him still. Jamie didn't close his eyes and noticed that Grant didn't either.

Jamie touched his lips lightly to Grant's and moved them back and forth, side to side, slowly, gently. He took the time to feel the softness and sweetness of Grant's lips. The man had a mouth made for kissing.

Jamie touched his tongue to Grant's top lip and tasted him, delighting in Grant's small gasp. He continued to take his time, moving his tongue all around Grant's mouth, top to bottom lip, teasing the corners, gliding across the seam. The whole time he looked into Grant's eyes, loving the look of wonder there.

He finally eased back a little and moved his thumbs over to smooth over Grant's moist lips, caressing.

"You like kissing…" Grant observed.

"I *love* kissing…you." Jamie leaned in again, moving his thumbs out of the way to allow his tongue to push its way inside this time. Grant groaned aloud and brought his arms up to clasp Jamie's neck, holding him close. Both pairs of eyes closed now as they gave themselves up to sensation. One of Jamie's hands went around Grant's head, and he fleetingly thought how wonderful Grant's hair felt on his fingers. He moved them through it, massaging Grant's scalp as he continued the marauding kisses.

There was nothing gentle about them. Grant mimicked Jamie's move, put his right hand on the back of Jamie's head and moved his fingers through Jamie's short hair. Neither could ever say how long they sat there, lips fused together, tongues moving from one mouth to the other. Grant caught on quick and he soon had his tongue searching Jamie's mouth, taking in flavours and textures that had his breath coming faster.

They went from hard searching kisses to soft sweet caresses, but the connection was never broken. It was as if now that they'd gotten the chance to get this close, they were reluctant to move apart. Grant's hand moved down to the back of Jamie's neck and rubbed and squeezed causing goose bumps to appear on Jamie's skin. Jamie followed suit, doing the same to Grant who moaned right into Jamie's mouth.

Finally, Jamie thought he should pull away, if only to get a good breath. Grant had other ideas. He allowed Jamie to ease back from his mouth, but he kept his arms tightly around him, not allowing him to move away. Jamie was fine with that. He just leaned in and put his face into Grant's neck and held on. They sat for a few moments as their breathing calmed and their hearts slowed a little.

"I never knew I could feel like that," Grant said, his lips moving against Jamie's shoulder.

"Good, yeah?" Jamie said without taking his face away from Grant.

"Oh my God, yeah," Grant was able to say, squeezing a little with his arms. "I love how you feel in my arms. I wish I could hug you harder, but this right side can't handle it. It feels great, though."

Jamie hugged him a little harder, being careful of the injured areas. He finally eased back and looked at Grant. When he saw how full and bruised-looking Grant's lips were, he wanted them again.

"Damn. Do my lips look like that?" he laughed.

"You mean a little puffy and red…and sexy as hell?" Grant asked.

"Yep. Man, you can kiss!" Jamie said, meaning it as a compliment.

"I think I was inspired."

"I'm a lucky man." Jamie finally let go of Grant and sat back on the couch beside him. He turned, putting one leg up, so he could sit sideways and face Grant.

"I think we need to take a little break. I don't think I've ever gotten quite so much just from kissing. You take my breath away. I'm glad we're on the same page," Jamie told Grant.

"Well, I can tell you I've never felt like that. I know it's odd that I've gotten to this age without really doing anything...sexual, but..."

"Hey, there's not a measure that says you have to have a certain amount of experience by a certain age. You're just where you should be for you." Jamie wanted to disavow him of the notion that there was anything wrong with him.

"Okay. I see that. I just hate that I feel so backward and awkward. I don't know what I should be doing. I don't want you to lose interest because I'm so lacking in..."

"Dude, don't even. Do you think I'm interested in you just for sex? I'm almost insulted." Jamie put his left hand to Grant's face, turning him and holding onto the side of his head as he continued. "I think you're intelligent, interesting, and sexy. I like spending time with you, talking with you, learning about your life and dreams. I like sharing my dog with you. I want to share my home with you for as long as you need it and maybe longer if you want." He watched Grant swallow past an obvious lump in his throat.

"I'm sorry. I told you I'm so new at this. I'll do and say things wrong. That's what I meant, not that I think you're just looking for..."

"An easy fuck? A slut? Someone to take the edge off?" Jamie supplied. "That's not what you are, Grant. You're a friend first, a sexual interest next, maybe a lover sometime soon. I'd like us to see if we have what it takes to make a relationship. We'll see. I want you to really hear what I'm saying. Relax. There are no demands, no expectations, just a lot of hope, on my part, at least."

Grant reached up and covered Jamie's hand on his face. "Jamie, I'm right with you. I just don't have all the words. I'm not as...what did you call it? Swave and deboner?" He chuckled at Jamie's blush. "I've seen you interact with others and you're smooth. You know just what to say to make people feel good. You have your LOLs who love you, your colleagues think you're great. It's all because you have this open, easy way about you. I'm not like that. I've always been..."

"Alone?" Jamie supplied when Grant paused. "The question is, do you want to continue to be alone? Or do you want to be part of my life? You don't have to be like me, just be with me." Jamie waited after laying that all out there. The ball was definitely in Grant's court. His answer would set the way for them.

Grant leaned over towards Jamie and whispered, "Breathe."

Jamie didn't realise he was holding his breath.

"You have to know that I want to be with you," Grant continued. "I can't believe my good fortune. I know, finally, what I want out of life. You've opened my eyes. I'm firmly out of the closet, and it feels good, freeing." Grant ended by placing his lips against Jamie's in a soft sweet caress. Jamie gave back in kind. It was a beginning for them. They'd both declared that they wanted to be together. Said it right out loud and been accepted.

"It's probably a good thing that we have to go slowly because of your injuries. I won't freak you out by jumping you before you're ready, but when you are free of the casts and the pain, look out," Jamie promised, laughing at Grant's blush.

"I think I can handle that. I can live on your kisses until that time. It's not really fair to you, though."

"I thought we'd already established that I'm not looking just for sex. I'm loving being with you and letting things grow. Now, don't look down. I know *that's* growing, too. Of course, I'm hard for you. Hell, I've been hard many, many times thinking about you. It stands to reason that when I'm this close and you tell me that you want me, too, that I'd be that way again. Contrary to popular belief, a person can live without getting off every time they get hard."

"Tell me about it. But, hey, I don't see why something can't be done about it this time. Can I…I mean, will you let me…?" Grant turned red, evidently both with want and the embarrassment of not being able to finish his request. He knew what he wanted to do, it seemed, but he just couldn't put it into words yet.

"You can do anything you want, always. You don't need to ask permission to touch me. But you don't have to feel like you have to…"

"Now there you go, see? I don't feel like I have to anything. I want to touch you, see you, feel you. I want to watch you come on my hand. I want to see your face when you do," Grant said, enjoying the incredulous look on Jamie's face as he reached out for him.

"I thought you were supposed to be awkward and...backward, was it?" Jamie had only thought he was hard before. At Grant's words, his cock became rock hard and painful.

Jamie leaned over past Grant to the table and grabbed the couple of napkins he'd put there with the snacks. He dropped them onto the couch then took Grant's face in his hands again.

"You make me happy," he whispered, close to Grant's mouth.

"I haven't done anything yet," Grant said, right against Jamie's lips.

"Ah, you finally get my point," Jamie replied, right into Grant's mouth. He flicked his tongue against Grant's lips, slipping past them into the sweet haven waiting for him. Grant met his tongue and there followed a duel that had them both ready for more. Jamie slid his hand down and moved it over Grant's chest, feeling the hard thumping of his heart. Jamie knew his banged away just as hard.

Grant pulled back and said, breathing hard, "I never thought I'd like kissing so much. Lord, I love your mouth." There was a look of wonder on his face.

Jamie gave him another kiss just for that.

"I know the basics, but tell me what you like, how to make it good for you," Grant requested, smoothing his hand down Jamie's stomach to his waist.

"Honey, you're too caught up worrying about your lack of experience. Forget it. Touch me. That's all it's gonna take, believe me. I'm so hot for you, you're not going to get to where you need a special technique to get me off. Just. Touch. Me." He barely got the last out as Grant began to do just that.

He slid his fingers past the waistband of Jamie's loose denim shorts. Oh. God. Jamie leaned back a little, giving Grant more room to work. After a couple seconds it was obvious Grant needed help getting his jeans open. He couldn't get turned around enough to use both hands well, so Jamie reached down and got them open for him and sucked in a deep breath as Grant took his cock into his hand.

"Oh, Jamie. You are gorgeous. I love the way this feels," Grant said, his eyes never leaving Jamie's groin. He moved his hand down and back up. He wasn't pumping, trying to get Jamie off. He was exploring, enjoying the act of learning the textures and what made Jamie jerk or gasp or sigh. He loved every bit of it. The responses he got from Jamie led him in the right direction. He learned that there was a spot right under the flared head that made Jamie respond sharply every time it was grazed. Touching the slit, wet with clear liquid, made Jamie suck his breath in and hold it.

"Come on, gorgeous, give it up for me," Grant said, still watching what he was doing with his hand. Hearing Grant say that was all it took. Grant's eyes widened, and he smiled as Jamie jerked and hot pulses of cum covered his hand. He kept it moving, gently still, but not stopping until Jamie slumped against the side of the couch, shaking and sucking in air.

Grant was elated. He'd done a good job. He'd made Jamie happy, made him shudder and sigh with completion. He felt like he'd performed something great. He moved his hand and found the napkins, cleaned Jamie up, then turned a little to look at Jamie's face. He smiled. Jamie's eyes were closed, and he was smiling. Grant leaned, winced a little as his shoulder was pulled, but kept going until his lips were against Jamie's.

Jamie felt Grant's lips on his and opened his eyes to find that Grant was right there. He opened for Grant and let him in. They kissed, wet and wild, for a long time. Eventually, Jamie caught on that Grant was in an awkward position and was probably hurting himself just to keep the connection going. Not good. He reached up and put his hands on Grant's shoulder and eased him back. He liked the look of awed accomplishment and joy on Grant's face. He didn't like the look of strain that he was sure Grant was unaware of.

"Baby, careful. Don't hurt yourself. Oh my God, you melted me," he said then switched to caretaker mode. He glanced down and quickly put himself back into his pants. He looked carefully at Grant. Yep, he appeared a little worse for wear. He'd done a little too much.

"Okay, darlin'. Here's the deal. When was your last pain pill?" When Grant told him he'd had none today, he said, "I'm gonna get you some Advil. You're hurting, I can tell. We'll get you a couple of pillows to make you comfortable until they take effect. We'll have a little snack, then it's time to go back."

"I'm fine, really. I hate being so..."

"Shh. I know. Relax. Come on, this is what I do. This is the first time you've been out, and we kind of forgot you're one of the walking wounded...so to speak. My bad. I let you go too far, but I was such a goner once you touched me." Jamie stopped a second and looked at Grant before adding, "And by the way, you can lose any anxiety you might've had about your performance. Your natural curiosity will carry you a long way." He laughed as Grant blushed.

Jamie brought a couple of pills and pillows and got Grant settled. He took the juice back to the kitchen, got some cold from the fridge then they sat and nibbled and drank and just looked at each other.

Jamie leaned over once and whispered to Grant, "Next time, it's your turn."

He laughed aloud when Grant ducked his head. He might be embarrassed, but he was excited, too. Jamie could tell.

Suddenly, they both jerked as Brit went crazy barking. He ran to the front door and jumped up then over to the side window. He was crazed, snarling and barking. Jamie sprang up as Brit ran towards him and looked up, still barking.

"What the hell? Whatsa matter, boy?" Jamie went straight to the front door and opened it to see what had Brit so excited. He heard a car squealing away as he opened the door but was unable to get a look at it. He hurried out and hopped down from the porch, trying to get a glimpse of the speeding car, but it had already turned the corner and was gone. He glanced around at the yard, the front of the house, and his car in the driveway.

"Damn it!" he yelled and sprinted over to it. All four tires were slashed

"Jamie, what's going on?" Grant called from inside.

Jamie ran back in, knowing Grant would be frustrated that he'd had to sit on the couch while Jamie checked out the situation. He grabbed his cell from his pocket as he came back in.

"It seems someone has slashed my tires...all of them," Jamie said, dialling 9-1-1. "Any idea who might have done it?"

"One."

"Yeah. I'm calling the police and reporting it." Shit. After they answered, he went through the necessary explanations and agreed to wait for an officer.

"Grant, this is getting scary," Jamie admitted. "I'd almost forgotten about Donnie since we haven't seen or heard about him lately. I don't like knowing he knows where I live." The thought that it might be someone else didn't even occur to him. This had Donnie written all over it. Sneaky. Hateful. Now, he remembered Grant saying Donnie had been around right before Jamie had picked him up today. God, had he followed them here? Been outside the whole time? Jamie got madder with each thought.

"I'm so sorry. You know this is because of me, right?" Grant said, a little bit of apology in his voice.

"Don't even! He's always been slime. I've always detested him," Jamie said. "He may have stepped up his game since you showed up, but it's all on him, not you. I wouldn't trade knowing you for anything."

There was a knock on the screen door, and Jamie turned to see one of his neighbours.

He went over and opened the door.

"Tony, hey. What's up?" Jamie said.

"I thought I'd tell you I saw a guy out at your car while ago. He took off, laying rubber, down the street.

When I looked again, I saw your tires. Man, that sucks." Tony shook his head then dropped a bigger bomb. "I've seen him here several times, so I didn't think anything when I saw him by your car at first."

"You what?" Jamie freaked, yelling. "When? How many times have you seen him? How long has he been coming around here?"

Tony's eyes got bigger as the questions flew at him.

"I'm getting a really bad feeling here. I thought he was a friend of yours since I'd seen him around," Tony explained. "I guess I've seen him five or six times over a several month period. I'm sorry. I didn't know there was anything wrong."

"Nah, I'm sorry for yelling. Hey, will you tell the cops what you told me?" Jamie asked, then admitted. "I think I have a bona fide stalker. He's been hassling me at work, and it came to a head recently. I called him on it, and now, he's retaliating." He looked up when he heard a car pull up out front.

"Uh, Tony, this is Grant. Grant Stevens, this is my neighbour, Tony Howard," he introduced the two as he waited for the officer to approach. He tried to throw in a little humour. "Talk amongst yourselves."

He met the policeman, Officer Johnson, at the door, stepping out to introduce himself. He pointed to the car with the flat tires and started explaining. They walked over to the car and he watched the officer walk all the way around it from a distance.

"You mentioned that you might know who did this," Johnson said.

"Yeah, come on inside, and I'll fill you in. There's a bit of a story," Jamie said, holding open the door for him.

He introduced the officer to the other two men. As he finished explaining what Grant was doing there, it occurred to him that he had to call the centre and explain what happened and that he would get Grant back as soon as he could.

Tony offered to take them both back when they were finished with the officer. Jamie took him up on it. He finished his story and said he'd better call his road service and have his car towed so he could get new tires. Officer Johnson asked if he'd wait on that until he had someone out to see about getting Donnie's prints off the car. They'd have a better case if they could prove what they all thought to be true. The officer suggested that Jamie get a restraining order against Donnie. He explained how Jamie would have go through the court system to obtain it. The police would serve Donnie with the order demanding that he stay a certain distance from both Jamie and Grant. Jamie almost said no, but the more he thought about it, the more he decided it would be a good idea.

Right now Grant was vulnerable. He couldn't protect himself if the need arose and Jamie didn't want Donnie anywhere near Grant.

"Does Grant live here?" the officer asked.

"He's going to be, really soon. When he's released from the centre, he's moving in here so he can continue therapy for a while. Donnie's jealous of Grant, and I'd like to do it if Grant could be covered in the order, too. Donnie could try anything at any time, and until Grant is on his feet again, he's in a vulnerable position."

Officer Johnson said for Jamie to be sure the order covered what he wanted, Jamie, Grant, and his property. Since it was Jamie's property that was vandalised, it had to start with him.

"Thanks for being so understanding, sir. I appreciate it," Jamie said, really meaning he was grateful the guy wasn't homophobic. Some would be in this situation.

"No problem, I have a brother who is, shall we say, 'of the persuasion'." Officer Johnson headed for the door. Tony had gone to get his car. Jamie's was dusted for prints and several were found above each tire on the body of the car. Jamie had no doubts about whose they were. Next, the service showed up, got his car up onto the back of the truck and took it to have new tires put on.

"Whew! Never a dull moment around you." Grant winked as he said it.

"It's funny. My life has been so dull and routine for years. Then, all of a sudden, you come into my life and there's excitement galore," Jamie teased him right back.

He could see that Grant was getting ready to apologise again, so he leaned down and shut his mouth the best way possible. Before they could get something really interesting started, they heard a beep outside. He backed up, reached down to help Grant up from the couch and got him into his chair then they headed out to meet Tony and go back to the centre.

Tony was going to drop off Jamie to pick up his car later. He waited while Jamie took Grant into the centre. Jamie wondered what the next step would be. Would the police find Donnie and arrest him? Jamie had no doubt that the fingerprints on his car were Donnie's. Would that be enough to keep him away from them? He got back into Tony's car, and they headed for the garage.

Very, very late that night his phone rang. Jamie rolled over to grab it, noticing that it was after three in the morning. He snatched it up and answered. It was Jackie, who was working the night shift that week.

"Jamie, I thought you might want to know about this. There's been a…sort of an incident here. Grant's okay, but…"

"What! Tell me, Jackie." He sat up, running his hand over his head, his heart nearly pounding out of his chest.

"I'm trying to. There was a small fire in the trashcan in Grant's room. The alarm went off, and everyone was freaked out for a while and…"

She got no further before Jamie broke in. "You're sure Grant's okay? A fire? What the fuck? How could there be a…?" A really sick feeling washed over him and he began to shake.

"There was a cigarette in the can. It smouldered for a while then caught. It was on the other side of the bedside table so it wasn't visible, and Grant was asleep so he didn't notice it at first. I think he was using the call button just as the alarm went off. He's fine, I swear it, Jamie."

"I'll be there in a few minutes. Hey, will you tell Grant that I'm coming in? Quietly? Just let him know." He knew Grant had to be freaking out, knowing it was probably Donnie. Grant didn't smoke. Hell, how stupid was Donnie, anyway?

Jamie was up, dressed, out, and on his way in a matter of minutes. There were very few cars on the road at three in the morning. He'd always thought it was kind of slow when he got off at eleven, but this was like...eerie. It was because of that feeling that he noticed when a car came up behind him—close behind him. He slowed to let the guy know he was a little too close. That didn't help. He couldn't tell what kind of car it was, but his mind immediately went to Donnie. Surely not!

He sped up and went tearing into the lot of the centre, watching to see if the car followed him in. It didn't, but it slowed and crept along in front of the lot before speeding away. All he could tell was that it was a dark car and pretty big. Shit. Shit!

He hurried inside and onto Grant's hall. He saw Jackie at the desk, obviously waiting for him. She came up to him and touched his arm. "Take it easy. Don't freak out and cause a bigger problem here. I know you all are special friends, but you *don't* want to create too big a scene. You know what I mean?" She looked at him closely. She was letting him know that she had figured out the relationship he was forming with Grant, and it was okay with her. "It's okay, Jamie. I'll cover for you, but don't get in trouble, okay? There might be some here who wouldn't handle it well."

He stopped a second, taking her hand, pulling it to his mouth for a quick kiss. "Thanks, Jack. You're the best." He meant it. She'd been a good friend for a long time. It was good knowing she accepted him. But, right now he had to see Grant. He had to.

"They've moved him across the hall. Luckily, that room was empty, and they've already got all his equipment set up. He's come a long way, hasn't he?" She smiled at Jamie as they walked down towards

Grant's new room. "He's almost ready for outpatient therapy. That's great."

Jamie nodded, absentmindedly. God, what if it had been worse?

As they reached the door, Jackie looked in and saw that there was a tech in there with Grant. She called to the young girl and sent her on an errand. Looking at Jamie, she whispered, "I'll cover you. You've got about four or five minutes before someone comes back. I'll knock four then two to let you know someone's coming. There've been people in and out for the last hour. It's finally slowed down."

Jamie threw her an appreciative look and stepped in Grant's room, firmly closing the door. Grant looked up, and the look he gave Jamie warmed his heart.

"Oh," he said, softly. "Oh, Jamie. You came. What are we going to do? You know I don't smoke. It wasn't me. It had to be..." Grant got no further. Jamie had reached his bedside and bent to place his lips right over Grant's. Grant whimpered into his mouth, raising his left arm to hold onto Jamie's neck, holding him in place. Like he was going to move? He braced himself with one hand on the bed by Grant's head and the other held the side of Grant's face.

He put all his fear, hunger, need, and anger into that kiss. He thrust his tongue inside and moved it in and out, hard, taking and claiming with fierce emotion. His advance was met by equal need on Grant's side. They were breathing hard, but both refused to let up.

They expressed their feelings in that kiss. There was relief that Grant was all right and abject fear as they both thought about what might have been. Play moved back and forth from one mouth to the other, mashing lips, nipping with teeth, and tangling tongues until at some silent signal they both eased it down.

Jamie wouldn't let go. He rested his forehead against Grant's but didn't take his lips away. It was awkward, but he couldn't move just yet. He opened his eyes and saw that Grant's were open, too.

Grant's hand moved on the back of Jamie's head, caressing, calming. Jamie moved his against Grant's face, doing the same, smoothing and just loving on him a little. The moment was as necessary as the kiss had been. This was a silent affirmation of the feeling between them. They were a unit, facing a threat and getting through it. They were both angry and afraid, but they were also thrilled at being together, at having found each other.

Four knocks then two.

Jamie reluctantly pulled away and forced himself to let go of Grant. He sat down in the chair by the bed, and when Jackie and a nurse walked in, they seemed to be just talking.

"So were the police here, too, or just the fire department?" he asked, looking at Jackie.

"Both. Grant was adamant that he had not been the one. Well, of course not. Like he'd smoke then be able to toss the cigarette over the table, hit the hidden can and cover it with one of the hospital gowns? I know you played basketball, Grant, but that would be quite a feat, huh?"

Grant smiled at her, nodding. He looked calmer now. His eyes weren't as wide and glassy as before. When Jamie had come in, he'd looked like he was ready to jump out of his skin.

"Can you tell me the officer's name?" Jamie asked Grant.

"Uh, yeah, it was..." He paused a second, and Jackie supplied the answer.

"Thomas, Office Mark Thomas was his name. He took a good look around and talked to the men from the fire department a long time. I've got his number if you want," she finished, looking at Jamie.

"I do. I want him to report this to Officer Johnson who was at the house earlier."

"What for? I mean, why was there an officer at the house earlier? Jamie, what's going on?" Jackie asked in concerned.

"I'm sorry, I haven't had a chance to tell you. Someone slashed all four of my tires this afternoon while Grant was at my house."

Jackie gasped and put her hand up to her mouth. "Jamie!"

"I know. They checked for prints on it and got a lot. We both think it's Donnie. Hell, my neighbour—you remember Tony? He says he's seen the guy around my house several times." Jamie nodded as her eyes nearly popped out of her head. He continued, "This is getting way out of hand, Jack. It's gone from silly harassment to wanton endangerment. Soon as we have proof, we'll press charges."

Then something else occurred to him, "Actually, I think someone followed me to the centre tonight."

"What?" Grant jerked upright, then winced. "Are you sure?"

"Pretty much. I was pretty much flyin' low to get here, and this car came up behind me and stayed right with me, too close. Every time I slowed down, he did, too. I sped up, so did he. When I got here he held back and didn't follow me in, but he slowly drove past the place before taking off. Big, dark car. I was a little freaked but more worried about getting in and finding out what had happened here."

"That's weird, Jamie. You think it was...him?" Grant asked.

"Him? You know who did this?" Jackie asked. "Wait, you think it was Donnie?" Jackie's eyes widened, and she took a step back. "That's bad, Jamie. What are you going to do?"

"Tell the police what's going on. Take a few more precautions. Be on the lookout 'til the police stop him," Jamie said, knowing it didn't sound like enough.

"Maybe I shouldn't come to your place when I leave here," Grant suggested. "If I backed off, maybe he'd..."

"No way! I am so not letting him get in the way of...of us," Jamie exploded, not caring that Jackie heard. "Just give up? Let him win?"

"I'm sorry, Jamie. I know. It's not what I want to do," Grant admitted, following Jamie's lead and ignoring that Jackie stood there listening. He seemed to be getting comfortable with his realisation of his life as it was now. Jamie felt a sense of pride in Grant's ability to accept this new aspect of his life. Admitting and accepting the fact he was gay and it wasn't going away was a big step.

"Well, forget it. Donnie isn't going to force us apart. He just has two people to contend with instead of one now," Jamie said. "We'll let the police handle him. But I will see a lawyer and find out what I need to do to get that order Officer Johnson was talking about. I want you protected. We'll be fine." He prayed it was true. Who knew how far Donnie would go?

Chapter Five

No one could find Donnie. The police and Donnie's dad, Bob, were looking. Jamie and Grant weren't, but they were watching out for him. They hoped they wouldn't see him, actually, but were afraid that, of all the people actively searching, they'd be the ones to see him next. It was nerve-wracking not knowing when it would be. Jamie felt sure Donnie would show up again.

The rehab centre was a new facility so it was equipped with security cameras outside. They didn't have them installed on the inside, but there were several around the perimeter of the lot. Donnie hadn't been seen on the cameras from that night, but his car was shown leaving the lot. It was big and dark.

Bob had called both Jamie and Grant and apologised profusely for the problems his son had caused them. He was, of course, hoping there wouldn't be a lawsuit. They hadn't even thought of doing something like that. Hell, it wasn't Bob's fault or that of anyone at the facility.

They requested that Donnie be banned from the centre and told Bob they'd tried to get a restraining order against Donnie. This, of course, could not be done if the police couldn't find him. Jamie had gone to a lawyer who'd taken him to a judge who'd agreed to issue the order, but it had to be served on Donnie and he was nowhere to be found.

Jamie and Grant both thought that Bob looked haggard. No wonder! His son was being hunted, literally, by the police with an eye to charging him with several felonies. The fire he'd started here could have killed several not just harassed Jamie and Grant. That took it from small to big time in the eyes of the law. They knew from the prints that he'd vandalised Jamie's car. Jamie and Grant had then admitted the subtle threats he'd issued before he'd started the physical harassment.

Not everyone knew the reason Donnie had done the things he had, but they knew they were to report it if they saw him anywhere nearby. The very best care was being taken with Grant. It was like he'd become a celebrity in the little arena of the facility and was seldom alone. He told Jamie one day, as they were sitting outside after a therapy session, that he was getting a little paranoid about it.

"Everyone likes you. What happened has you in the spotlight, so to speak, and people are now more aware of you. They like you and don't want anything more to happen to you." Jamie smiled at Grant, who looked a little embarrassed. "'Course, it might have been a direct order from Bob. He's gone way out of his way to make the rest of your stay here safe and easy. You've got what? About a week before you're released to my care? I'm having new locks put in and a security system, too." Jamie's frown was fierce now. "I won't live in fear of him showing up. I'll be ready if he does, but I want a little warning."

Grant looked worried. "I hate that you are going to all that expense because of me. I could…"

"Hey, relax. Remember what Tony said that day? Donnie's been sneaking around my house for months. Shit, that gives me the heebie-jeebies just thinking about it." Jamie actually shuddered as he thought about Donnie skulking around his house when he wasn't there. What if he'd tried to do something to Brit? "I'm doing it for me as well as you, okay? Wanna go out for lunch tomorrow?" Jamie asked, changing the subject and knowing he'd get a bright smile.

"Can I?" There it was, beaming. Grant was pretty much propelling the chair by himself and was about to get out of it and advance to the crutches. His shoulder would be sore, but if he used them sparingly and was very careful, he'd be allowed to get around a little without the chair.

"Yeah, I checked. I'm on spring break at school so I have some time to get things ready at the house, and I thought I'd run by here and pick you up for a little outing. I'll have you back for your therapy session. I'll take you to my favourite place. It's very small and funky, but the food is great."

"I'm sold. Let's do it. I'm ready to get out of here for good, and I'm really looking forward to going to your house. This whole thing has been pretty surreal, ya' know?" Grant looked at Jamie with his head cocked to one side as he asked.

"Good or bad?" Jamie was anxious to hear the answer.

"Oh, definitely, *mostly* good, Donnie notwithstanding, I have so much to be thankful for here. I made it through a horrible wreck. I'll eventually be fine. I've met someone I am coming to care for more and more. I have a wonderful place to stay while I finish recovery. It's good."

"I'm glad you look at it that way." Jamie smiled, wanting to reach out and touch Grant so badly. "You could be wanting to get as far away as possible since I have Donnie looming on the horizon." Jamie was sure Donnie would be back around again. "If it wasn't for his obsession with me, you wouldn't have to worry about being safe."

"Jamie," Grant began, very serious now, "I've enjoyed the times we've been able to spend together. I can't wait to spend some real quality time with you. It's worth anything to me. Alone is not all it's cracked up to be, compared to being with…you." He finished on a blush.

Jamie loved it. He ached to touch him. Just put his hand out and run his finger down Grant's pink cheek. Draw it down his neck, slide it under his shirt, ease it down to caress—

Whoa! Not the time to pursue that journey in his mind.

"I'd love to be kissing you right now," Grant surprised him by saying.

"Oh. Wow. Right back at ya," Jamie answered. "And a whole lot more."

"Soon, yeah?"

"Oh, yeah," Jamie promised.

Love, Jamie

****

Grant was coming home today. That's how Jamie thought of the transition from the centre to his house. No matter where the relationship went, right now it felt like he was bringing his lover home. He hoped Grant felt the same.

Jamie had gotten up early and run with Brit, then he'd gone through the house again, making sure everything was ready for Grant. He'd put a couple of rails in the bathroom to make things easier for him there. The security system was in and functioning, and the new locks were installed.

He'd gotten lots of healthy food in, as well as some of his favourites to share with Grant. He whistled as he headed for the door to pick up his new roommate. Brit barked happily, keeping pace with him, thinking he'd get to go along.

"Sorry, boy, not now. I'm going to get Grant. Yeah, your new buddy. He's moving in here with us. Hold the fort 'til I get back," he said, not thinking there was anything at all odd about talking to his dog.

Soon Jamie returned with Grant and the few things he had with him.

Brit was barking furiously as he opened the door and helped Grant inside. He stayed back, though, until Grant was settled on the couch. Then he went over, tail wagging, to be loved. Grant complied, and they passed a few happy moments while Jamie took Grant's meagre belongings to his room.

"Wow," he said, coming back into the room. "I can't believe you're finally here. It seems like I've been waiting forever to get you alone." Jamie plopped down on the couch within easy reach of Grant.

"So, what are you going to do about it?" Grant asked, with an honest to God, come-hither look in his eyes. Well, all right!

"That was an invitation if I ever heard one," Jamie laughed as he leaned to put his lips to Grant's.

"You're right," Grant whispered into his mouth. There followed many minutes of soft sighs and moans of pleasure. Jamie was thrilled to be back where he'd wanted to be for so long. He knew Grant liked to kiss, and he loved the feeling of Grant's full lips moving on his. Their tongues tangled and teased, showing their delight in being back together. It was heady stuff. Jamie moved closer so he could embrace Grant.

"This okay? I'm not hurting you?" he asked, against Grant's lips.

"No, don't stop, please. I've waited my whole life for you, for this," Grant said, making Jamie's heart swell.

They continued to kiss, letting their feelings escalate to the point of hunger.

"Jamie...Jamie...I need...more," Grant mumbled.

"Me, too," Jamie answered, readily. "How about we take this to my bedroom? I'd love to lie down with you and feel your whole body against mine."

"That sounds wonderful. Help me?" Grant indicated the crutches that Jamie had placed at the end of the couch.

Jamie helped him manoeuvre through the house to his bedroom. Grant declined a stop in the kitchen and the bathroom.

"Just you. I just need you," he said, leaning back on the facing of the door to the bedroom. He looked into

Jamie's room and saw that the bed was really large. He hadn't paid any attention to it when he'd visited before.

"That is some bed." He sounded enthused.

"Has to be. I'm a big guy with a big lover. I'm glad I paid for the king now," Jamie said, putting his hands on Grant's hips from behind and giving him a gentle push, indicating that he should go on in. He kept his hands on Grant until he stood by the bed. He helped as Grant turned and sat, handing the crutches to Jamie to put away.

"Do you have a favourite side?" Grant asked.

"Whichever side you're not on. I just want to be beside you — when I'm not under or over you, that is," Jamie said, watching the blood rush to Grant's face. "Scare you?" he asked.

"No, not at all. Excite me? Now that's another story altogether." Grant scooted back so he could swing his legs up onto the bed, still a little clumsy with the cast on his ankle.

"How long 'til that comes off?" Jamie asked. "Have they told you yet?"

"They just say soon. It was evidently a really bad break. Lots of pins and screws and such." Grant didn't really want to talk about his recovery.

Jamie went around the bed and crawled on from the other side, sliding all the way over to Grant. Suddenly, he burst out laughing.

"What?" Grant asked, perplexed.

"Look," Jamie said, pointing to the side of the bed. There stood Brit with his head on the side of the bed, looking for all the world like he wanted to join them for some good lovin'. So not going to happen right now.

Grant snorted out a laugh. "Do you let him on the bed?"

"Not usually, but he's confused with you being here and in my bed," Jamie said, then pointed at Brit.

"No, Brit. Not now. Go on out and leave us alone. We'll play with you later," he said, pointing to the door. Brit tilted his head as if he couldn't believe he was being banned. "Go on now," Jamie said again, and Brit sighed deeply and padded to the door. They both chuckled as he stopped and looked back as if to say, "Are you sure?"

"Brit!"

He left then.

Grant turned to Jamie, still smiling. Jamie scooched closer to Grant and reached to cup his face.

"Hey," he said, quietly.

"Hey," Grant answered, huskily.

"I feel like I've waited for this moment forever."

"You?" Grant replied, as if to say, "What do you think about me?"

"Grant, we don't have to do anything you're not ready for. I want you to tell me if I do anything that makes you uncomfortable," Jamie said, suddenly nervous. It came home to him that while both had been anxious to be alone and get something started, Grant was still new to all this. He didn't want to freak him out.

"It's okay. I feel a little nervous knowing I'm finally going to follow through on some of my fantasies and, hopefully, yours," Grant said, reaching over to put his hand on the side of Jamie's face. "You don't have to worry about me. I'll let you know if I'm uncomfortable. Frankly, I can't think of anything you'd do that I wouldn't want." He slid his hand up to run it through Jamie's hair, loving the feel of it between his fingers.

"Let's just shut up and go for it," Jamie suggested, sliding his fingers to Grant's mouth and tracing his lips. Grant pushed his tongue out and licked them then sucked one into his mouth. He curled his tongue round and round that finger, as if it were something much larger. He looked right into Jamie's eyes as he went down on his finger.

Jamie's breath hitched, and he shuddered. Grant didn't seem like a novice. Jamie thought about Grant applying that action to his cock and moaned at the image in his mind. He decided his finger had been loved enough and pulled it out of Grant's hot, wet mouth and replaced it with his tongue.

He pushed up on his elbow so he was over Grant, and he eased him down to the pillow then put some of his weight onto Grant. He knew where Grant was likely to still be sore so he aligned himself accordingly. He received a grateful sigh as Grant took his weight and embraced him. There was strength in that hug today.

He pushed his hard cock against Grant's hip on his left side and began to rock gently against him. Grant gasped into his mouth and tightened his arms around Jamie.

"Feels good…you feel good on me…wanted to know…how…how it would feel with you in my arms, pushing me down…" Grant managed to get the words out past Jamie's lips as they continued the kiss. Jamie thought it felt pretty damn good, too. He put a little more of his weight onto Grant, testing to see how much he could handle.

"Yeah, that's it. More…" Grant said, pushing up a little, trying to turn more into Jamie's body. Jamie helped him, pulling a little on his shoulder to ease him onto his side. Grant sighed as they faced each other. Grant eased his right arm over Jamie and pulled. Jamie helped again by pushing right up against Grant in a full out embrace. He put his arms around Grant and held him close, lining their torsos together to put their straining cocks together.

"Oh. Oh, Jamie, yeah…" Grant moaned, beginning to rock against him. Jamie slid his hand down Grant's back to his ass and pulled him in tighter. He held him still, not wanting him to hurt his hip. Jamie did all the work now, humping against Grant, making both of them pant with need.

"God, I'm gonna…oh…Jamie…so good…gonna come…make a mess…" Grant rambled.

"It's okay. Do it…got a washer. Come on. Let go, Grant," Jamie said back, loving the fact that Grant was about to lose it. He pushed a little harder against him, and they both came, each shouting the other's name. Grant dropped his head to Jamie's shoulder and breathed deeply for a few minutes. Jamie just moved his hand over Grant's back and shoulders, easing him down.

"That made a good impression, didn't it?" Grant said, obviously embarrassed.

Jamie was having none of it. "What, that we both got off just by touching each other? I think it was great. Did any of it feel bad to you?"

"No! It felt great. I just thought you'd want me to be…" He trailed off, not really knowing how to finish.

"I want you to be you. I'm not looking for a performance," Jamie said, looking at Grant. He pulled his hand around and pushed Grant's face up to look at him. "Seriously, anything we do together is fun and feels good. There are no expectations. We touch, we kiss, we caress, fondle, tease, tempt, play—it's all good, Grant." He watched carefully, as Grant took in his words. "If you want to kiss me, do it. Touch me. If you want something from me, ask. Just ask, and I'll do anything you want…any time."

"It's all so new to me, but I'm not freaked out or anything. I like everything we've done."

"Good. If you want more, tell me. If you want a break, let me know. A blow job? I'm your man. Whatever you want."

"Uh…could we get cleaned up? This really feels yucky." Grant moved his soggy groin against Jamie's, grimacing. "Then maybe…we could spend some time just touching, tasting, looking, exploring. We'll go wherever that takes us."

"I'm all for that. Let's hit the bathroom, then some naked time here sounds really good. I like the way you think." Jamie smiled, planting a quick kiss on Grant's lips and rolling over to get off the other side of the bed.

When they got to the bathroom, Grant saw all the things Jamie had fixed up just for him. He thanked him with another kiss. He heard a rustling sound.

"Whatcha got there?" he asked as he leaned on the door facing and looked at Jamie.

"Wanna take a shower?" Jamie knew the idea would have a lot of appeal.

"You're kidding?" Grant's eyes lit up.

"Honey, showers are one of the joys of being gay, didn't you know that?" Jamie teased.

"No, I wasn't aware, but I'm willing to learn," Grant teased right back. The rustling, he saw, was a trash bag.

"We're going to secure this tightly around your leg and, with a lot of help and holding from me, you can stand in the shower. Sound good?"

"Good? Lord, it sounds wonderful. All of it, the shower, the help and the holding..." Grant looked like he was envisioning heaven. It was a good look on him.

Jamie went about getting things just so for the two of them — towels, clean clothes for later, shampoo and soaps, loofahs and cloths. He turned around and found Grant struggling to get off his shirt. He went to help. He pointed to a stool he'd brought in and Grant hobbled over to it. He held on as Jamie took off his pants off, gingerly easing them past the cast. He had Grant sit down, and he wrapped the bag around his cast then looked up from the floor. It was a beautiful sight. Grant was very tall and well built. He'd lost weight, Jamie was sure, but he looked absolutely delicious.

"God, you look sexy," he told Grant as he stood.

"Me? You...you're the one who's pure eye candy, and you know it," Grant answered him.

"No, I don't, but I'm glad you think so." Jamie moved close to Grant and smiled when Grant was not slow in figuring out what to do. He reached to tug the shirt out of Jamie's shorts, and Jamie bent so he could pull it off. He stood still as Grant took care of his shorts and soggy briefs.

He reached to help Grant stand by the stool and said, "Here we go, first time." It was obvious from the look in Grant's eyes that he knew what Jamie referred to. It was the first time they would touch each other, head to toe, naked, skin to skin. Grant let Jamie see the excitement in his eyes. It was matched by Jamie's expression.

Jamie stepped in and put his arms firmly around Grant and heaved a giant sigh as they came together. He held on tight, making sure that Grant was steady on his feet and because he just wanted to. He lined them up perfectly and just held on for a few minutes.

"So, what do you think? You know, you'll always remember this. The first time you were ever like this. It's special."

Grant put his head on Jamie's shoulder and held on, his arms around Jamie's waist and shoulder. He moved his lips over Jamie's neck, sliding over to the top of his shoulder, leaving kisses and licks and nibbles as he went. Jamie shuddered and moved his face against Grant's neck.

"I like this. It feels good, like having you on top of me felt awhile ago," Grant said, easing back a little to look at Jamie's face. "I never really thought about how this would feel. I mean, I guess I just pictured the sex, not the journey. I'm lucky," he finished.

"You are?" Jamie smiled into his eyes.

"Yeah, I could have fallen for someone who didn't have the patience and the desire to take things slow and let me enjoy getting to all the stages instead of just...well, wanting the sex," Grant said.

"Oh, baby, don't doubt that I want the sex—and soon—but see, I'm enjoying your journey, as you put it, too." Jamie was serious. He was horny as hell and wanted Grant with every breath he took, but he also enjoyed showing him the ropes and make it good for him.

"Let's get in the shower, before I forget what we're supposed to be doing here," Jamie went on to say as it became obvious from the heaviness below that both of them were ready for more than foreplay.

They carefully manoeuvred into the shower stall, easily large enough for the two big men. Jamie manhandled Grant into a position under the spray after he got it just right. He propped him up against the wall, and showed him how to hold the rail he'd put in, making him steady.

If anyone heard the sounds that followed they'd have thought the two men in the shower were having full out sex. There were groans and moans and sighs and even a whimper or two. Jamie took great delight in washing Grant from head to toes. He used the time to explore which areas were especially sensitive and which ones got the biggest responses. He smiled as he catalogued them in his mind for later use. He took his time, soaping and smoothing and massaging a little. He had Grant turned into a near puddle before it was over.

"Jamie, my God, how do you expect me to keep standing? Don't you want me to...?" he started, but Jamie interrupted.

"Nah, not today. But one day, definitely, I'd love to have you wash me. Right now, you can just watch. I'll be really quick so we can get out and you can rest a little. We don't want to overdo on your first day here." He was quickly scrubbing away as he talked. He made short work of what had taken him quite a bit longer on Grant. Once he was clean, he stepped out then reached to help Grant get out safely. He had big towels ready for them. He helped Grant to the stool and got him settled. He kept up his ministrations by quickly drying Grant's hair then smoothing the towel down his body, again not missing a single spot. Grant watched him closely, face flushed and eyes bright. Jamie took the bag off Grant's leg, glad to see it wasn't wet.

He stood right in front of Grant and proceeded to dry himself. He didn't mind admitting that he made a bit of a show of it. He rubbed his hair roughly, to dry it, knowing the motions made his cock swing and bump against his legs. He knew Grant was watching, and he made it good for the man.

"You are a mean, mean man," Grant teased. "Look what you've done to me."

"Why, Mr. Stevens, what do you mean? Are you saying you like what you see?" He shimmied a little as he put the towels in the hamper in the corner and came back to Grant. He laughed right out loud. Damn, life was good sometimes.

"I more than like what I see, Jamie. I want what I see—as you can tell."

"We do seem to have a matching problem," Jamie said, reaching to slide his finger from the base to the tip of Grant's erection. Grant sucked in his breath and put his hand on Jamie's waist to hold on. His cock curved up, touching his stomach now and leaving a little trail of liquid shining there.

Jamie touched his finger to it, bringing it to his lips to taste. Obviously he didn't have to worry about Grant being clean. He knew Grant had no experience, but he also knew they would play safe until he was tested again. Jamie was clean and had always been, but it was a point he would make. There would be no sex without condoms.

"Damn, you're sexy," Grant said, shaking his head. "I keep saying that. It must be true."

"I'm not the only one," Jamie said, taking Grant into his hand and squeezing just a little. "This is beautiful."

"Really? I never thought about it. But now that you mention it, I like the way yours looks, too. It's bigger than mine. I want to touch," he said, looking at Jamie as if for permission.

"I told you that you don't have to ask. Touch," Jamie offered, and added, "and I may be bigger, but yours is longer, I think." He kept moving his hand on it, base to tip. "I can't wait. You're going to turn me inside out with this, aren't you?" he asked, looking at Grant and smiling at the look on his face. It was one of mixed eagerness, shock and embarrassment.

Jamie stood still and let Grant reach out to touch him. He spread his legs a little, inviting exploration. He knew they should go back to the bedroom, but sometimes you just didn't want to leave a situation that was going so well.

He couldn't help the shiver as he felt Grant's hand on him, tracing top to bottom, circling, holding, squeezing and studying. He sucked in a deep breath as Grant took his finger and pressed into the slit on the end of his cock. Joy blossomed as Jamie watched the dawning expression appear as Grant realised that was something that turned Jamie on. Jamie thought he was the lucky one.

Finally, he pulled away, despite the rough sound Grant made when he lost his hold on Jamie. Grant looked up, his eyes half-closed and showing definite need.

"Let's go back to my room, lie down, and either finish this or take a nap. You've got to be tired. I'm not going to be responsible for any problems with your recovery." Jamie pulled on Grant's hands, helping him stand. He gave him the crutches and went slowly beside him, bringing the clean clothes into the room and putting them on top of the dresser. Watching as Grant went to the side of the bed and eased down onto it, he saw the wince as his hip made contact with the bed. Jamie went and helped Grant swing his legs up and made his decision. He went around the bed and slid over to settle next to Grant.

"I think a nap would be the best idea. You need to rest, and I'm always ready for a nap and a cuddle. Come on. Here's another joy to learn about," he said, opening his arms and taking Grant into them. They settled with Grant's head on his shoulder, their torsos touching, legs tangling. He could feel Grant taking deep breaths right against his neck.

"Oh my God, this is wonderful," Grant enthused. "I never dreamed something this simple would feel so good, so…rich."

"I know. It's good. Shh…you relax and sleep a bit, okay? Here's Brit, come back to see if he's welcome now." He raised his head to look over at Brit and said, "Go to your corner, boy. We'll see you later. Maybe we'll cook out tonight." Brit padded over to his corner, where his big bed waited and settled down after a couple of circles around it to make sure he had just the right angle. Grant was already closing his eyes, and he became a dead weight on Jamie's side. Grant had been so right. This felt better than good, it felt right. He tightened his arms a little, soaking up the feeling of having Grant right where he wanted him.

Jamie watched Grant, sleeping hard, obviously worn out. He chided himself for being lax with his care and too eager in his affection. They needed to take it slow and let Grant recuperate before trying too much. Deciding to get up and putter around while Grant slept, he eased off the bed, dressed, and motioned to Brit to be quiet and follow him out.

He took Brit out back and played with him for a while, enjoying the spring breeze. He'd already made sure the grill was ready for cooking out later. Like a good little Harvey Homemaker, he'd also cleaned the patio table and chairs and thought Grant would enjoy eating outside tonight. It would be very romantic. They'd get a lot of talking done, getting to know each other better. He grinned, just plain happy with the day.

"Now that's a sight," he heard from the back door. He turned his head and saw Grant standing there with the crutches. He was leaning on the door facing, and Jamie wondered how he managed to look so sexy like that.

"Hey, Sleeping Beauty awakes," Jamie teased.

"No fair, wasn't there supposed to be a kiss?"

"Well, come on out here, and I'll take care of that for you. Can you manage that step?" Jamie asked, sure that Grant could handle the one step down to his patio. He had a fleeting moment of thanks that his parents had put up a high privacy fence all around the back of the property. He and Grant could do anything they wanted and no one would see. Perfect!

"No problem. I feel way better, by the way. I'm clean, rested, and happy to be here," Grant answered, swinging down the step with no problem.

"That's what I like to hear," Jamie said, forcing himself to stand still and let Grant come to him. In just a few seconds, he had his arms full of happy, laughing man. He had one arm around Grant's waist and the other cupping the back of his head. Oh, yeah. Jamie took a few more seconds to look into Grant's smiling face before dropping his mouth over Grant's and giving him a proper wake up kiss. Excited, he put a lot into it and soon they were both fully up and awake. They pressed against each other and moaned as the kiss deepened and lengthened. Tongues talked and hearts listened as they moved from gentle teasing to serious to tender delight.

"Mmm," Grant said, "just what I needed. I gotta say, Jamie, I feel like I've finally found myself."

"You were lost?" Jamie said, deliberately misreading his meaning.

"No, not lost, just not aware. I've been living in a sort of vacuum," Grant tried to explain his thoughts. "I've been alone because I wasn't into women and was too scared to admit I was into men."

Jamie started to interrupt, but Grant put his fingers over his mouth to stop him. He went on to say, "I was, Jamie. I can see it now. It became clear to me when I met you. I was instantly interested and comfortable with it…with you."

Grant's fingers moved from Jamie's lips to glide over the features on his face. He traced Jamie's brows, his cheek and jaw, and back to linger on his lips. "That grew, Jamie, until I had no doubt that it was real. The funny thing is, I thought I'd be freaked out about it, but I'm not. I'm just happy, deep down, full out, happy. It's you, just you, that makes me comfortable admitting that I'm gay. I'm so lucky that you feel the same way." Leaning, he put his lips over Jamie's and moved his fingers to the pulse thumping hard in Jamie's neck.

Jamie groaned and met Grant's pure emotion with honest need. He was thrilled at hearing those words from Grant.

They were close to the same height which felt good to Jamie. They fit perfectly as they held each other, kissing passionately.

Finally, Jamie pulled his head back and laughed into Grant's eyes.

"You make all my good intentions go right out the window," he said, with a rueful grin on his face.

"What?" Grant asked, head tilted to the side, in obvious confusion.

"You got just a little too sore and worn after our time earlier and I'd decided we should try to cut back on the physical stuff until you were a little better."

"Hey, it was just a kiss. You're not going to tell me we can't kiss?" Grant sounded so upset Jamie had to laugh.

"Oh, definitely not saying that. No, not saying that at all," Jamie laughed, reaching to kiss Grant again. It was hard to hold the kiss with both of them laughing.

They finally gave up, and Jamie pulled a chair out for Grant to sit at the table with him.

Grant took a moment to look all around the yard. "This is really nice, Jamie. Everything's beautiful, and the fence makes it so…private."

"Yep, we can do anything we want to out here," Jamie smiled over at him. "Do you like working in the yard?"

"I've never had a chance, really, but I've always thought it would be cool to have a garden. I'd love to grow vegetables and maybe some bright flowers. Does that sound terribly gay?" Grant asked, looking down instead of at Jamie.

"First of all, I don't think you can sound *terribly* gay. I've been thinking more and more about putting in a garden. The idea of growing things sounds great to me. Wanna help me do it this year?"

"I'd love to. It sounds like fun, a great way to share time and chores, and you get food out of it. What could be better?" Grant looked excited at the idea.

"Great. We'll look into it. We'll decide where would be the best place to put it, what kind of things to plant, and what we'll need to get started. What kinds of flowers interest you?

"I don't know, those bright red things in pots for the porch maybe. There was a place close to where I grew up that had a huge bush thing with so much colour. I don't know what it was, though. Oh, and there was a row of these, like…flowers on a stick." He looked embarrassed.

"Don't think I've heard of those. No problem, we'll have fun checking that out. We'll look online and see if we see something like that, then we can go to the nursery near here and try to find them." Jamie waved his hand towards the backyard and said, "Look around here and tell me where would be a good place for the bush." He watched closely as Grant looked around the yard. He suddenly realised that if Grant answered these questions the right way, he'd be committing himself to a long stay. He held his breath and waited.

Grant did look around the yard then turned to look at Jamie, noticing how still he was. There wasn't anything slow about Grant. He reached across and touched Jamie's hand.

"Breathe, Jamie," he said, looking right into his eyes. "I think over in that left corner would be great. What do you think?"

Jamie turned over his hand and took Grant's, holding it, sliding his fingers in between Grant's. "I think that would be perfect. What colour?" His eyes never left Grant's. They were both aware that they were agreeing to be together through the summer or indefinitely.

"Dark red," Grant answered, finally.

"I'm beginning to get that you really like red, huh?" Jamie teased.

"Yep. What about you?"

"Any colour of green," he answered quickly.

"All-time favourite TV show?" Grant asked, moving his fingers against Jamie's.

"Queer as Folk," Jamie answered.

"I never saw that," Grant admitted.

"Not a problem, I've got all five seasons on DVD. Yours?"

"West Wing. Favourite singing group, current?" Grant asked.

"Daughtry. Yours?"

"Hey, ditto. Favourite movie?"

Jamie thought a minute, said, "The whole Lord of the Rings series."

"Good answer, mine would be Independence Day."

"Yeah, that's a good one. What about country music? Like any?"

"Garth."

"Yeah, can't beat that. I like Rascal Flatts lately, too. Junk food?" Jamie asked, keeping the game going.

"Rice Krispie Treats. Love 'em." Grant answered, eyes twinkling.

"Buy 'em or make 'em?"

"Buy 'em, but I'd love to make some."

"We can do that." Jamie smiled at him, totally enjoying himself.

"Yours?" Grant asked.

"Nacho Cheese Doritos. Man, if I were ever stranded on a desert island and could only have one food, no contest, gotta have 'em."

"You're a nut."

"Yeah, I am. But this is fun, let's continue playing while we get supper going. Wanna? I've got steaks, fries to bake in the oven, and stuff for a salad."

"Sounds fabulous. How can I help?"

"I can set you up in the kitchen with the veggies for the salad. I'll get the grill going and take care of the steaks. The fries can take care of themselves in the oven. We'll eat out here. We're good to go."

"Do we have dessert?" Grant asked.

"Nope, but we obviously have a sweet tooth," he teased. "I thought maybe we'd go for a short drive and get some ice cream later. Favourite flavour?" Jamie asked, holding open the door for Grant to go in.

"Rocky Road." Quick answer.

"Pralines and Cream," Jamie replied.

"Apples or oranges?" Grant asked.

"Oranges."

"Yep."

"Cake or pie?" Jamie asked, reaching to take out the veggies from the bottom drawer of the fridge. He turned to find Grant enjoying the view. He smiled and pointed his finger at Grant.

"Caught ya lookin'," he said, sliding his haul on the table. He turned to get a cutting board, knife and two big bowls, one for garbage, and one for the salad.

"Busted...and cobbler, any kind of fruit cobbler. Mmm." There was a look of ecstasy on Grant's face. Jamie made a mental note to get an easy recipe for them to try out soon. He'd ask Jackie.

"Cake, yellow cake with chocolate icing. Man, I could eat a whole one, double layered." There was no doubt of it when they both heard Jamie's stomach growl loudly.

They both laughed and got busy working on their first supper together. Jamie reached over and turned on a CD player, and they both smiled as Maroon 5 came on loud and clear.

* * * *

Later, full and happy, they sat at the table, watching the stars come out.

"God, this is beautiful. I can't believe I get to be here, stay here, enjoy all this, and on top of it all, there's you." Grant said.

"Believe it, cause I feel the same way. Oh, look, someone's feeling a little jealous," Jamie said, pointing to Brit. "Although, I'm not sure who he's jealous of, me or you. He's pretty smitten with you, I think."

'Course, so was Jamie.

"Come here, Brit. I'll love on you a little. I've gotta save some for your daddy, though."

Jamie flushed, loving the words from Grant. He stood and cleared the table in just a few minutes while Grant and Brit rubbed and growled and laughed. Soon, he came back out and said, "We'd better get in gear, if we're going out for ice cream. Brit, you wanna go for a ride?" he asked, knowing how Brit would respond. He barked twice and went to stand at the door, as if to say, "What are you all waiting for?"

They both laughed and went in and got things put away in quick order, then Jamie grabbed the keys and they trooped out the front door to the car. Brit got in the back, as usual, and Jamie got Grant settled into the front.

"Best cruising music, windows down, music loud?" Jamie asked, starting the car.

"Mmm, Bon Jovi. Usher. Justin. Mary J," Grant supplied. It just so happened Jamie had a Bon Jovi CD handy. He pulled it out of the case, popped it in and off they went. Words weren't necessary as they drove around for a while, enjoying the warm night, the music, and the company. They ended up at the Dairy Queen and both decided on Blizzards. Grant ordered Oreo Cookie, and Jamie ordered Heath Bar.

They shared back and forth, trying to get the other to change their allegiance. It didn't happen. They both stood firmly by their original choice. They spooned them up, laughing and talking. Since they were parked at the end of the row and there wasn't another car close and it was dark, Jamie reached over and took Grant's lips in a sloppy, tongue tangling kiss.

"Mmm," he said when he came up for air. "They go pretty good together."

Brit barked from the back seat.

Okay, time to go.

Jamie headed out and asked Grant to choose something else to listen to on the way home. He was pleased when Grant chose Garth Brooks. They were happy with their world as they finally pulled into Jamie's driveway. As he put the car in park, he heard Grant gasp. He looked over, and Grant's eyes were huge as he pointed to the front door. Written in large red letters that were still running down the door were the words, *Motherfuckin' faggots live here.*

"Holy shit!" Jamie was furious. Grant was stunned. He craned his neck right and left, but saw no one around. It was nearly ten by now, and the neighbourhood was quiet.

"Jamie, what're you gonna do? Call the police again?" Grant asked, finally finding his voice. Brit was beginning to get agitated in the backseat, wanting out to check his domain.

"Wait a minute. I'm calling, and I'm gonna see if Officer Johnson's on tonight. We need him here. I'll see if he's available. You okay to sit there for a few minutes? I don't want to mess anything up before they get here." Jamie was so mad he was shaking. He reached for his cell and stared to call 9-1-1. Grant reached across the seat and touched his arm.

"I'm sorry, really sorry, Jamie." It seemed that Grant still felt like the mess with Donnie wouldn't be happening if not for his appearance on the scene.

"Yeah, me, too. But not enough to give you up, so don't even go there." Jamie took Grant's hand, brought it to his lips for a quick kiss, then dialled and waited to report the most recent vandalism. Luck was with them, and Officer Johnson was on duty. Dispatch said they'd radio him and send him over. They were to sit tight until he got there.

"Why can't they find him to arrest him for all these things, but he can come and go like this? You know it was him," Grant mused. The name wasn't even necessary. They both knew who'd done this.

"Yeah, I'd bet my last dime it was the smarmy bastard," Jamie answered and shook his head. "As to your question, I can't answer that. Bob hasn't heard from him. I know this is killing him. He knows what Donnie's done and that the police are looking for him. He can't deny Donnie's guilty, but he has no clue what to do."

Brit barked and whined to get out.

"Easy, Brit. Stay still just a little longer. We'll go in soon."

Grant unbuckled his seatbelt and turned a little in his seat, reaching to pet Brit as the dog put his big head between the seats. Brit was obviously upset. He clearly sensed something was wrong, and he didn't like it one bit.

Finally, they heard the police car drive up and park behind them in the driveway. They both opened their doors. Jamie came around and got Grant's crutches for him. He let out Brit but told him to stay so he wouldn't go up on the porch. They didn't know what else might be up there.

"Evening boys. I hear we've got more trouble," Officer Johnson said.

Jamie pointed at the door, and the officer looked then spat out, "Damn, now that's just not right. Wait here a minute while I look around." He started forward. Brit wanted to go with him so badly he shook where he sat. Jamie reached down and rubbed his head, trying to calm him. Grant leaned on the car, his crutches resting beside him. They watched as the officer moved slowly around the porch, checking for any other evidence of foul play.

"It's okay, guys. It looks like the graffiti is the only thing here. It's red paint not blood."

That hadn't even occurred to Jamie. He shivered and looked over at Grant, easily reading his look. He hadn't thought about that, either.

He gestured towards the door and waited for Grant to get the crutches under him. They started for the porch, meeting Officer Johnson on his way back to his cruiser.

"I'm going to get my camera and get some shots of this. You have a box you can cut up to cover it for the night until you can do something about it tomorrow?"

"Yeah, I'll find something," Jamie answered. "Is it all right to go in now, or should we wait?"

"Just for a minute," he answered. "Let me get a few shots, then I'll take a look around again. Can you get into the backyard without going through the house?"

"Yeah, there's a gate right at the end of the driveway. It's locked right now, but I can get you the key if you want to go through." The idea bothered Jamie. "You think he's still here, or that he did something else?"

"Never know. Best to check things out thoroughly," the officer answered, clicking away. He gave them the nod to go on in. After opening the door and carefully avoiding the wet paint, Jamie gave him the keys and showed him the one to the gate.

"Brit, go with Officer Johnson, stay with him," Jamie said and was pleased when Brit did just as he asked. Officer Johnson nodded, and they went around the corner of the house and Jamie and Grant went on in the front room.

"I don't know what to say. I hate this, Jamie," Grant said, walking slowly and clumsily over to the couch. He'd been moving so well earlier and now it seemed like this latest act of hatred had him out of sync. Jamie understood.

Before Grant could sit down, Jamie went to him and put his arms around him. Donnie, the dipshit, was not going to take their joy away from them.

"Hey. Don't let this get you down. We're stronger than he is. He's not right. I mean, there's something wrong with him," Jamie clarified.

"I agree, but I also think he's dangerous. What if we'd left Brit here? Would Donnie have hurt him?" Grant's mind was obviously coming up with awful scenarios.

Jamie thought it all out and answered the best way he could. "I don't know. Evidently, he's been here before when I was working and Brit was here. He'd have to be able to get in or into the back yard. It's not impossible, but it would take some doing. Are you worried about being here when I'm gone?"

"No, not at all. I'll have Brit here and the security system, and I have a phone. I'll practice using my crutch as a weapon," he was clearly trying to inject a little humour into his answer. It fell way short.

"Not even funny, dude. I'd have to kill him if he hurt you in any way."

"I feel the same way, Jamie. I don't know what I'd do if he hurt you."

"We'll hope the police find him soon. The charges are adding up—if we can even prove he did this."

"What about your neighbours? Do they know about you? Have you ever had a problem with them?" Grant asked, as Jamie finally let him go to sit on the couch. Jamie was pacing in front of him now.

"Good question," they heard from the front door, where Officer Johnson was coming in. "Looks okay out there. I relocked it. Great dog, by the way. He minds."

"Yeah, Brit's my buddy. Come here, boy. You can relax. We're all right." He patted his chest, and Brit put his paws there, standing as tall as Jamie when he did. He was a really big dog. Brit licked the side of Jamie's face. He got a couple of rubs then was down and going to put his head on Grant's leg for more. He was also a smart dog.

"About the neighbours...I don't know. I've never had a problem. I don't have a rainbow flag out front, but some of them know about my preference. Some of them are young, and I know them. They've seen me with guys a couple times. Not recently for sure, like not in a couple of years. I don't think it was one of them."

Grant spoke up. "I doubt it was. This is the first night that I've been here. It's not like they've seen us around a lot. I think it was Donnie. He'd know when I was released and could have been watching. When he saw us leave, he took his chance. It's creepy. The man's an honest to God stalker." He shivered from head to toe, obviously freaked out a little at the idea.

"Yeah, we could be a movie of the week," Jamie suggested.

"I agree with your thinking, but I thought I'd see what you thought about the neighbours," Officer Johnson said, running his hand through his hair in frustration. "Listen, get the stuff, and I'll help you cover this up so they won't all be reading it on the way to work tomorrow. Then make sure things are locked up right and tight tonight and don't worry anymore." He glanced from one to the other. "I'll drive by a few times before I go off duty, and I'll have the next detail do the same. I'll get this written up and get back to you."

Before long, there was a big piece of cardboard over the bottom half of the door where the words were and the officer had left. Jamie made a mental note to check with Tony tomorrow and see if he'd seen Donnie's car here earlier. The house was locked down, and the three occupants were settled into the bed in Jamie's room.

They'd made short work of getting ready for bed, and Jamie broke one of his cardinal rules and let Brit onto the foot of the big bed. Jamie and Grant clasped each other tightly, neither talking. They just held on tight while their brains were filled with worry and frustration. Grant was so tense that Jamie worried he'd be really sore tomorrow.

"Hey, relax, hon. Turn over and let me rub your back. You're so tense, I think you'd break in half if pushed too hard," Jamie said, easing back from him, giving him room to move. "We're both okay. We'll be fine. Let's not let him ruin our first day together. Come on, over now."

"Maybe I should rub your back," Grant suggested, though he moved as requested.

"I surely wouldn't say no. That's one of my favourite things. I love being touched, caressed, smoothed, massaged, loved on. I've missed being touched."

"Well, I guess you know I've missed it, never having had it." Grant wasn't whining, just stating the fact.

To Jamie, that was the saddest thing he'd ever heard. He thought about it, and it made a sad kind of sense. If Grant was alone all the time, he'd never known the joy of touching and being touched. Oh, he was in for a treat. Jamie set out to show him what he'd been missing. He could do this, knowing he was doing something good for Grant's recuperation. The fact that he'd enjoy the hell out of it was just an added bonus.

Grant was duly appreciative of the tactile expression of affection from Jamie. He moaned and sighed as Jamie moved from his neck and shoulders down his back. Jamie took care around Grant's hip but deep massaged his buttocks and the back of his legs. He was gentle with the right leg but spent a good bit of time, smoothing and relaxing the muscles.

He ended at Grant's feet, bending to kiss each toe, getting soft chuckles from Grant. He crawled back up and kissed the back of Grant's neck, moving his hand through Grant's hair, bending his fingers and scratching his scalp and tugging on his hair a little. He knew it felt great from the noises coming from the pillow. He thoroughly enjoyed making Grant feel good. He reached up to put a soft kiss on the side of Grant's face, lingering for a few seconds.

"You are in so much trouble," Grant murmured, sleepily.

"Why's zat?" Jamie asked, just as quietly.

"I'm never…going to want…to let you…get away…from me."

"I don't see that as a problem, Grant," Jamie said, lying down beside him, his arm reaching over and rubbing softly now over Grant's back, knowing he was about out for the night.

"Good…it's good…" Grant said and was gone.

Chapter Six

Jamie woke up lying on his side, Grant's breath on his shoulder blade. Grant was glued to his back, his sore right arm using Jamie as a pillow. Jamie smiled and opened his eyes. Brit was staring at him, making no sound, his head on the side of the bed.

"Hey, buddy. Wanna go out?" Jamie asked, whispering, and got a quiet whine from Brit instead of the usual loud bark. He was a smart dog. Jamie inched away from Grant, wanting him to sleep as long as he needed.

He let Brit out the back door and headed to the bathroom. He finished his business and brushed his teeth, looking in on Grant before going to the kitchen to make a nice breakfast for them. Plans changed when he saw that Grant was watching the door, anxiously. He relaxed when he saw Jamie at the door.

"Morning, Jamie," he rumbled in a deep, sexy, sleep-rough voice.

Jamie went in and leaned over the bed, dropping a kiss on Grant's mouth.

"Morning to you, too, Sleeping Beauty."

"And there's my wake up kiss. Mmm, you taste good. Let me get up, and I'll try to taste a little better than…ew…my mouth is yucky. Sorry." Grant looked embarrassed.

Jamie stepped back and let Grant get up, handing him the crutches. When they were both standing, he put his hands on Grant's shoulders and stopped him a second, leaning in for another kiss before Grant could back away.

"Don't care, but go ahead. I'll meet you in the kitchen. Sleep good?" he asked, as Grant headed for the bathroom. He was surprised when Grant stopped, turned around, and came back to him.

He leaned and put his mouth right beside Jamie's. "The best in months. Thank you for the massage. I was melted, and I will repay the favour soon." He pressed his lips to the corner of Jamie's mouth again and turned for the bathroom. Jamie stood and watched him move away. He shook his head. He had it bad for the man, he really did. He made himself go out and leave Grant alone.

He was in the kitchen banging around when Grant joined him. He hadn't heard Grant come in so he was surprised when arms came around him from behind. He set the skillet onto the back burner and turned off the heat, turning into the arms that were there for him.

"Hey." He smiled at Grant, pleased that he'd made the overture this time.

"Hey, yourself. I'd like that kiss now," Grant said, not waiting for a response.

Jamie barely had a chance to make a sound when his lips were totally taken. He opened for Grant's tongue, and they stood there in the kitchen, leaning on the counter by the stove. Hands roamed, lips nipped, tongues duelled and sighs erupted.

Grant played with moving his head this way and that, changing the direction of the kiss, now hard, now soft, but always hot. Jamie held on tight, thrilled with the way things were going. Neither seemed to care how long they stood there, Grant resting his weight on Jamie.

"Damn, you know how to kiss," Jamie sighed into Grant's neck when they finally came up for air.

"It's not from practice, that's for sure," Grant said, on a chuckle, clearly pleased at the compliment. "It has to be purely due to the feelings I have for you."

"Damn, you know how to tease," Jamie said, nuzzling into Grant's neck.

"Not teasing, Jamie. I mean it. This is not just a game to me, not a way to gather experience now that I've admitted what I want. It's not that I want to be gay. It's that I want to be with you." Grant appeared very serious in his need for Jamie to realise the honesty of his feelings.

"Hey, I'm sorry. I didn't mean you were teasing me like that. It just came out wrong. I feel the same way you do. To me, this is becoming a real relationship, not just convenience. Okay?" Jamie waited for his words to register.

Grant dropped his head to Jamie's shoulder and wrapped his arms tighter around him. He sighed and rolled his forehead back and forth on the top of Jamie's shoulder. "Don't mind me. I'll get used to things. I've never been in any kind of relationship at all. I'll need a little time to learn not to say things or take things wrong."

"You're fine, baby, just fine. You hungry?" Jamie asked.

"I could eat. What can I do to help? I don't want to be waited on," Grant said, looking around to see what Jamie had going.

"Set the table? I've got eggs to scramble and there are biscuits in the oven. That good for you?" Jamie asked.

"That's great. Coffee? OJ?"

"Definitely orange juice. I'll set it out, and you can pour it up."

They were soon working in sync, getting things done quickly, anticipating each other's moves. Grant was getting really good on the crutches. Sitting down to eat breakfast, they were interrupted by the phone. Jamie reached for it, easing back down with Grant.

It was Tony. "Hey, Jamie. I wanted to tell you. I saw that guy again last night. I got a call from my mom, and I had to rush over there. She'd fallen. She's fine, but I was in a hurry so I didn't even think to call you. I didn't get in 'til after midnight. I noticed this morning that you had something wrong with your door. Is everything okay? Did he try to break in?" It was a long speech from Tony, but Jamie didn't interrupt because he was sitting there with his mouth open in shock.

Jamie glanced at Grant who waited to find out what put that look on his face. It was probably hard to sit there, silent, but he did. He put his hand on Jamie's arm, and Jamie took it.

"Do you know what time it was?" Jamie asked.

"Yeah, cause of when Mom called. It was right after ten forty-five when I ran out of here. I thought you told me you were going to get a restraining order against him. Have you done it yet? Tell me, what's up this time?" Tony wanted info, and Jamie knew he wasn't just wanting the latest gossip. He was a good friend.

"He left us a message on the door. We'll have to try to get it off this morning." He squeezed Grant's hand. "And yes, I did. I went in and got it a couple of days ago, but the police have to take it to him and serve him with it. They have to find him first. The same officer came by and took pictures. Is there any way you could call the station and tell him what you saw?"

Tony said he only saw him getting out of the car, but he would call Officer Johnson and report it. Jamie thanked him and hung up.

"What?" Grant asked.

"Tony saw Donnie getting out of his car here last night a little after we left."

"Well, it's not like we didn't know. This way, we have more ammo against him, though," Grant said, pulling on Jamie's arm to draw him closer. He reached up to cup the side of Jamie's face and gave him a soft caress denoting encouragement and support.

They talked about what to do about the door and that Jamie had to work tomorrow but had the rest of today to spend with Grant.

"Wanna paint the whole door? Let's go to a hardware store and get some paint and just paint it. Make something good out of it. How about red, sort of in-your-face red?" Grant suggested with a smirk.

"I like it. It will look good with the rest of the house, and I like the idea of sort of flipping him off, so to speak. Let's do it."

"Let's eat our cold breakfast first. Mmm, delicious," Grant teased as he scooped up a bite of cold eggs and chewed. Jamie threw a biscuit at him, which he caught and put right back to Jamie's mouth. He took a bite and they shared a smile. Grant kept the biscuit, finishing it himself.

That's exactly what they did. They shopped and scrubbed and painted. Grant helped in every way he was capable. He painted the parts he could reach, held things for Jamie and helped clean up. He left Jamie putting things away and went into the kitchen to see what he could whip up for lunch. They'd been working hard. He found sandwich meat, lettuce, tomato, and pickles. Perfect. He went looking for chips and found...what else? Nacho Cheese Doritos, of course. He smiled and set about fixing them a quick meal.

Jamie came in and laughed when he saw the table set and ready. Grant was still putting together sandwiches, but he had the chips out in a big bowl and ice in the glasses. Good man.

"I like having you around," Jamie stated.

"Hey," Grant smiled, turning. "Did you manage to keep Brit out of the paint mess?"

"Yep. He didn't like the smell of the cleaner. What do you want to do this afternoon? Need a break? Wanna take a nap with me?"

"You don't take naps," Grant said, putting Jamie's plate down and going back to the counter for his own.

"I do now. We could rest, it'd be smart. Then, I thought we'd go for a ride this afternoon late. I'm not gonna live in fear of what that asshole's going to do next. Until we can fill our free time with much more...uh... energetic loving, we need to get out and do things. We'll consider it dates building up to the big time," Jamie watched to see what Grant thought of the idea.

"I like the sound of that. Uh, the more...uh...energetic loving? When do you think we could, you know, get to that?" Grant was blushing, but Jamie could tell he really wanted to know.

"I just *love* that you're anxious, Grant." Jamie winked, pulling out Grant's chair, putting it close to his. "You'll get a release from the doctor or your therapist. They'll let you know. In the meantime, we can do a little more and more along the way." He grinned over at Grant who listened raptly, never taking his eyes off Jamie's face. "There's lots of ways to show each other how we feel. Don't worry, we'll be fine. I'm enjoying the getting to know you part, and the slow build up is a turn on, too. 'Course, we may burn the house down when we finally get the go-ahead." Jamie was dead serious. He wanted Grant more and more each day, but he would not take a chance on hurting him.

"I am, too. I just want...more. I want you," Grant answered, making Jamie flush with need.

"Okay, that's it, nap time," Jamie said, standing and putting his hand out to help Grant up. "With much kissing, touching, and general making out."

"Oh, yeah!" Grant voiced his opinion of the plan.

"By the way, naps should always be taken naked," Jamie told in a very master teacher kind of voice.

"Oh, really? I never knew that before. Good to know." He laughed when Jamie couldn't keep a straight face.

They entered Jamie's bedroom, both laughing and holding onto each other. Jamie stopped and turned Grant into his arms, leaning back on the wall by the door. Grant made sure he was steady before putting both his crutches against the wall. Both arms went around Jamie, and he put his lips by Jamie's ear.

"I'm counting on you to help me to the bed," he said, ending his request by putting his tongue to the skin right behind Jamie's ear, smiling when Jamie shivered and tightened his arms.

"Don't you worry about that," Jamie said, turning his head, giving Grant better access to his sensitive neck. He moaned for his man, letting him know he was appreciative. His hands moved on Grant's back, one reaching under his shirt to get to his skin. He let his fingers move softly against the small of Grant's back, remembering that was a spot that got sighs and shivers last night as he'd passed over it. His instincts were right on. Grant sucked in his breath and wiggled closer, like a puppy begging for more scratches. Jamie kept it up as he turned his face to take Grant's mouth with his.

There wasn't anything slow and hesitant about this kiss. Grant opened up and took Jamie right in. He sucked on Jamie's tongue in an obvious rhythm that had both of them pushing their groins hard against each other. They moved together, getting hotter and more needy by the moment. Jamie grasped Grant tightly, glad the wall was behind him. He had to hold on to Grant and keep them both on their feet when all he wanted was to take Grant down to the floor.

Finally, Grant pulled back and put his face into Jamie's neck and tried to get back his breath.

"Please tell me you won't ever get tired of kissing me." Jamie didn't even mind that he sounded like he was begging.

"Not a chance."

"Mmm, good."

Grant pulled back his head, smiling at Jamie. "You said something about a nap…with benefits." He laughed at Jamie's eager expression.

Jamie helped Grant over to the side of the bed and proceeded to undress him. He went around the bed, undressed and slid in beside him. Just like clockwork, Brit put his head on the side of the bed by Grant, looking hopeful. Grant turned to Jamie.

"No way. Brit, either go to your bed or get out of here. We need some time without doggie love right now." Brit, looking dejected and unloved, turned and walked out slowly. This time he didn't even turn to look back at them.

"Jamie, is he…?" Grant obviously fell for the act, which was worthy of the Doggie Oscars.

"Don't even. You know he's not neglected." Jamie laughed at Brit's acting ability, but he wanted Grant to himself right now. "You and I have plans, dog-free plans. Come here. It's time to see how far we can go without causing you any pain."

"Mmm, wha'da'ya have in mind?" Grant turned to face Jamie.

"Well, last night I spent a lot of time getting to know your back side—and lovely it was, too. Today, I think I'd like to become a little more familiar with your front side. Work for you?"

"Yeah, but what about you?" Grant felt that things had been decidedly one-sided.

"What about me? You're free to do anything you want to my body—after I get better acquainted with yours, that is" Jamie wasn't into self-denial, but he really did want to get his hands—and his mouth—on Grant.

"Mmm, okay." Grant eased back down onto his back and waved his arm down his body. "Knock yourself out."

Jamie snorted a laugh and leaned over to drop a kiss on Grant's breastbone.

"You're a goof," he teased.

"Your goof," Grant said, waiting to see how Jamie would respond.

"My goof. Yes, mine."

Oh, Grant's look said that he liked the way Jamie had responded. He liked it a lot.

"Will you lay on top of me, all of you?" Grant asked, looking into Jamie's eyes.

"Are you sure? I mean, hip, shoulder, everything okay?" As soon as Grant had asked, Jamie had wanted that more than anything.

"I think so. Just try. I want to feel you, pushing me down into the bed. I want to hold you in my arms, see what it feels like. Please." Grant, this time, didn't seem to mind the pleading note in his voice.

Jamie wasn't about to make the man beg for something they both wanted. He'd be super careful, and at the first sight of a wince or gasp, he'd retreat.

"Here goes...or should I say, here I come?" Jamie leaned up on his elbow then pushed up to his knees and put one leg over Grant's body, making sure he avoided the sore hip. He put his arm over and put his weight on hands and knees. Lowering his body slowly, he eased down until he touched Grant from top to bottom. Grant shifted a little, getting a nicer fit with their legs, then he put his arms up around Jamie and pulled him tighter to his chest, taking the weight Jamie still held onto with his elbows on the bed.

"Ohhhh, oh, Jamie. That's what I'm talkin' about. You feel so good on me."

"Does it hurt anywhere? Tell me the truth now, Grant. I couldn't stand to hurt you," Jamie was torn between enjoying the feeling of being in Grant's arms and worry about causing him harm.

"No pain, I swear. Just feels...so...good," Grant said, moving his hands on Jamie's back now, one riding low, cruising over Jamie's hard, round butt, obviously loving the way the muscles tightened as he kept up the caresses.

Jamie relaxed and left it up to Grant to tell him if something wasn't right. He felt free now to focus on the thrill of the moment. Putting his lips to Grant's neck, right below his collarbone, where it would be hidden by his shirt, he began to suck hard, wanting to put a mark on Grant, wanting to claim him.

Grant gasped and pushed his hips up against Jamie's, his muscles clenching as the sting hit him. If he felt any pain in his hip, he covered. Jamie felt him relax. It was clear he wasn't giving this up. Grant hummed deep in his throat as Jamie finally pulled back to look at the spot he'd made on Grant's skin.

"Sexy…" Jamie murmured, looking at Grant from about an inch away.

"Yeah? Want a matching one?" Grant seemed excited by the idea of doing the same thing to Jamie.

"Hell, yeah. Want you so much," Jamie responded. He raised up a little and put his neck and chest within easy range of Grant's mouth. He gasped as Grant latched on and before long he had a matching mark on him.

"That's cool. We match. Almost like a promise ring ceremony," Grant said, teasing Jamie.

"Yeah, I promise to make you feel as good as I can for as long as I can. Now behave, and let me play a little, then it's your turn. Deal?"

Grant nodded, his eyes slumberous, never leaving Jamie face as it moved down to glide over his chest. Jamie gave him a lesson in his body's responses. Lips on his nipples made him warm all over, a tongue on his nipples made him hot, and teeth on his nipples made him gasp and moan. A tongue teasing his naval made him harder than a rock and a chin bumping the tip of his erection had him calling out. When Jamie took his cock in his hand and licked it from base to tip, Grant thought he'd died and gone to heaven. But he was wrong. That came when Jamie took it between his lips and moved down, taking as much of it into his hot mouth as he could.

"Oh…oh God, Jamie…oh…that's…mmm…" He couldn't seem to come up with words to tell Jamie how good it felt. Jamie knew anyway. Grant started to raise his hips again to meet Jamie's mouth, but stopped, presumably to keep the hip from hurting. Jamie caught on and pulled off and looked up at Grant.

"Pain?" He kept his hand moving on Grant, not leaving him wanting, but he would have an answer.

"Not enough to have you stop. I'll be still," he admitted. At Jamie's glance from his groin to his face, he swore. "I promise. Please, don't stop."

"'S okay, baby. I won't leave you like this. Just be careful." Jamie went back to making Grant fly. Soon, he pulled off again, knowing Grant was near. He leaned further down and licked and sucked on Grant's balls, his hand still moving on his cock. Grant shouted, and Jamie kept it up 'til Grant was through his orgasm. He kissed the skin of Grant's thigh, lapping up the crease that ran between leg and groin. He smiled as Grant shivered and gasped. With his other hand, he rubbed the cum into Grant's stomach, making lazy patterns in the moisture. He smiled as Grant laughed.

"What are you doing? Finger painting?" Grant asked.

"Maybe. Want me to make you a smiley face?" Jamie offered.

"You already made me a smiley face," Grant said, putting his hand on Jamie's head, smoothing it over his hair and curling it around the back of his neck. He put pressure on Jamie, showing he wanted Jamie to come back up to him.

Jamie put one last kiss onto the scar on Jamie's right groin, then, putting his weight on his knees, he moved back up. Instead of settling on top of Grant again, he slid to the side. When it looked like Grant would protest, he pointed his finger and chided him. "It's too much, Grant. You need to rest. I know that hurt you some, and I shouldn't have even done it, but I wanted to make you happy."

"And you did. God, you did. I'm going to do the same for you. Don't tell me I can't," he said, determination in his voice. He turned and scooted down so his face was level with Jamie's hard cock. "I'm fine like this. Please, let me, then I'll rest. I promise. Jamie, I want to taste you. I want your cock in my mouth."

Well, hell. When he put it like that, how could Jamie, or anybody for that matter, resist? He nodded, vowing to himself he'd keep a close eye out for any sign of pain or awkwardness from Grant.

It was clear that Grant had been paying attention or had thought about this a lot. He could have given classes. He took Jamie's cock into his hand and, in one move, had swallowed well over half of it. Jamie nearly shot off the bed.

"Oh, baby, damn. You're good. Yeah, like that." Jamie watched as Grant pulled off then licked around the flared head, paying close attention to the spot right under the bottom, making Jamie groan. He seemed very interested in the large vein going down the underside, tracing it with his tongue, flipping it back and forth all the way down and back up. Using the same action on the very tip, Grant paused to push into the slit at one point, garnering another gasp from Jamie.

Grant rested his chest on Jamie's hips so he could use his left hand to hold Jamie's cock. He'd moved a little to the side so he was almost perpendicular to Jamie. Grant used his other hand to move up and tease Jamie's nipples, knowing how sensitive his own were.

Jamie knew he was going to blow in a few seconds. He'd wanted this for so long and Grant was showing no backward behaviour as he'd feared. The man had Jamie tied in knots.

Jamie reached down to pull Grant off his cock, putting his hand over Grant's and helping him give it a couple of hard pulls then he was shooting straight up towards his chest. Grant looked from Jamie's eyes to the tip of his cock. He looked so pleased with himself that Jamie fell right then. He knew he'd been halfway in love with the man already. Grant's eagerness to please and the obvious happiness he got from Jamie's response, pushed Jamie that last little way. He wouldn't tell him and take a chance on scaring him off, but oh, yeah, he was a goner.

Jamie raised up and helped Grant get settled again. He scooted to the side of the bed, going to the bathroom and getting a washcloth. He got it wet and brought the warm cloth back to clean Grant's stomach, leaning to give it a lingering kiss, then he turned it over and cleaned his own on his way back to toss it into the sink. He hurried back to Grant.

He slid in beside his lover and lay on his side, head resting on his hand.

"So, proud of yourself?"

"I gotta say I am. I wanted to make you feel good, and I think I did."

"Ya' think? You could teach class, Grant. See, what'd I tell you? You don't have to worry about anything.

It's all just doing things for each other, making your guy feel good, teasing, touching, tasting, aching, loving. It's all good. You are one sexy man. I'm one *lucky* man." Jamie leaned to plant a kiss on the tip of Grant's shoulder.

"Jamie?" Grant paused.

"Yeah?"

"I'm happy." Grant looked stunned for a moment, before going on. "For the first time in my life, it feels like I have this light feeling in my chest, my heart is racing, and I look at you and just melt." He couldn't seem to help the smile that split his face "I'm happy. I've just been going along and living life until now. You make me happy. Please don't let me go," Grant said, closing his eyes now, afraid of Jamie's response to his sappy comments.

"Well, now see, I was just worrying that you might get away from me. It looks like we're both happy right where we are." He watched as Grant opened his eyes, happiness just shining out of them. "Let's keep it this way, despite the fact that your life is in limbo, 'til you're better. Despite the fact that we have a crazy stalker leaving us love notes and various acts of vandalism. Despite that fact that we can't have full out sex for a while yet, I'm just as happy as you are." He winked down at Grant who watched him closely. "We're a couple of happy fools aren't we, considering all the 'despites' in that speech?"

Grant smiled up at Jamie, reaching up to caress the side of his face. He slid his hand to the back of Jamie's head and pulled him down for a sweet, soft kiss. As Jamie pulled back, Grant yawned.

"Mmm hmm, I'm with you. Nap time for happy boys." They snuggled close to each other and were soon breathing deeply, heads close, bodies touching, hearts beating together.

* * * *

All was quiet on the Donnie watch for a couple of weeks. Jamie and Grant fell into a routine of work, therapy, studying, and exploring...each other. Grant helped Jamie study for his classes. Jamie helped Grant with his exercises. Grant played with Brit, kept the house clean and had easy meals ready when Jamie got home. They both took great delight in learning all the ways they could express themselves physically without causing damage to Grant's injuries.

Grant met a few of Jamie's friends. They both talked with Officer Johnson about any progress finding Donnie—none but the police were still working on it.

When Grant had been with him for three weeks, and Jamie had the weekend off, they decided to have a cookout and invite some of Jamie's friends over. It was also a celebration of Grant's getting his cast off the day before. He was still supposed to use the crutch for a while, but he was so much better, he forgot it half the time.

Grant was nervous about meeting Jamie's friends en masse and it being obvious they were a couple. He wasn't nervous about being outed. He was actually fine with that. He told Jamie he just wanted them to like him and think their friend had chosen well.

Jamie came into the bedroom and saw Grant.

"Dude, you look good enough to eat," he said, ambling over to stand right in front of Grant.

"You hungry already?" Grant teased.

"For you, always," He leaned in and took a quick kiss. They heard a knock at the door, which was open as they expected many to arrive right about now.

Grant pushed against Jamie, not wanting to get caught.

"Hey, guys? Where's the action?" Tony called.

"Little does he know, huh?" Jamie teased as he turned and they went out to meet the first of their guests.

There was a steady stream after that. Soon the house and the backyard were teeming with Jamie's friends. Jamie had introduced Grant, each time with his arm around his waist, letting everyone know they were definitely a couple. He began to relax as all of them seemed to accept Jamie's choice and were ready to get to know him.

* * * *

A couple of hours later, the party was in full swing. There were several areas around the backyard that were set up for groups to relax, eat and talk. Most of the guys knew Brit, and he went around from group to group, getting lots of love, but not the food for which he was hoping.

Jamie manned the grill and Grant moved back and forth, usually anticipating his needs. They made a good team, a fact that had been commented on more than once that night. Grant was thrilled every time he heard that.

"Hey Jamie, when're you gonna eat?" someone yelled.

"Soon, I'm almost done here. Anybody need anything else?" he asked generally. There was a chorus of negative answers so he began to shut down the grill. The last thing he'd done was fix food for himself and Grant. They headed over to one of the groups that had a couple of empty seats. Just as they settled in, someone yelled at Jamie.

"Jamie, dude, what's the matter with Brit?" There was a note of concern in the voice.

Jamie and Grant both whipped their heads around towards the voice and immediately rose when they saw Brit against the fence by the front gate, vomiting and heaving. Jamie ran with Grant hobbling not far behind him. Others headed over. As they neared, Brit went down. His legs just crumpled under him, and he hit the ground.

"Brit, hey, what's—shit!" There was a white foam around Brit's mouth, and he began to convulse.

"Brit!" Jamie yelled, fear and pain evident in his voice.

Grant looked around, trying to find what Brit had eaten. No one here had been feeding him. They'd all been here before and knew not to fill him up. Jamie was at such a loss for a few moments as to what to do that Grant took over.

"Jamie, can you lift him? If not, could someone help him? I'll get what we need from the house and meet you at the car." His hand rested for a moment on the back of Jamie's neck. "There're a lot of cars behind you, but you can just drive across the yard. I'll sit in the back and hold him." He turned to their friend and neighbour.

"Tony, can you stay here and make sure no one messes up this area? You know Officer Johnson, so can you call this in? Also, there's a number by the kitchen phone for the vet. Can you call and tell them we're coming in with an emergency?" Grant was already moving towards the house as Tony nodded his assent.

Grant headed out the front door with his and Jamie's wallets and the car keys. He had the door open and was settling himself into the back seat when Jamie and another man, whose name escaped him right now, made it to the car. They grunted as they managed to place Brit into Grant's arms. Brit wasn't moving now, though he *was* breathing, barely. Grant was scared and knew Jamie had to be out of his mind. What the hell had happened?

The ride to the vet was a nightmare. He heard Jamie making noises in the front seat and didn't know if they were from anger or fear. He wanted to say something to help ease Jamie, or touch him somehow, but he didn't want to distract him. As it was, Grant wasn't sure they stopped at lights or stop signs on the way. He just knew it was a very fast trip. They screeched into the parking lot, and Grant was glad to see Brit's vet standing in the doorway, waiting for them.

The door was opened at his side, and Jamie and the doctor reached in and managed to get Brit's lax body out and onto a waiting gurney. Jamie stopped on the way in and turned back to Grant. He waved Jamie on in and took his time getting out of the car, getting the keys, gathering their belongings and locking the car. He went into the waiting room, wishing he could go back with Jamie and Brit.

He looked up when the door to the back opened, and Jamie stood there, his eyes haunted, gesturing for him to come on. His heart thudded at the look on Jamie's face. He grabbed his crutch and hurried over and through the door. Brit lay on a table under a very bright light.

"Do you all have any idea what he ingested?" the vet asked, working over Brit's body. Brit already had a tube in his mouth going down his throat, and the vet was taking blood as he asked.

Jamie started to answer but had to stop and clear his throat, shaking his head. Grant took over for him again, giving him time to gather himself.

"Not really. We were cooking out, but everyone knew not to feed Brit. He'd been going around to all the different groups, but I didn't see anyone give him anything. He just started throwing up all of a sudden..."

Grant trailed off and put his hand on Jamie's back, rubbing.

"It's obviously some kind of poison. It'll take me a little while to find out what kind. It would be easier if we had a better idea what it was," the doctor said as he continued to move around the table doing different things to Brit. Jamie stood and shook. Every once in a while, he reached out as if to touch Brit but stopped short afraid to follow through.

"It's okay, Jamie, go ahead. He needs your touch," the doctor said, observing one of Jamie's failed attempts to reach out to Brit. "I have to tell you we're fighting an uphill battle here. His vitals are really down, and he's having a hard time hanging on. Touch him, talk to him, anything to help," he finished, urging Jamie to let Brit know, even subconsciously, that he was there for him.

Jamie choked for a second, scared, hurting. Grant took him by both arms and put his face right into Jamie's, ignoring the doctor nearby.

"Suck it up, baby. Brit needs you now. You can lose it later, I promise," Grant swore. "I'll be right there with you. Right now, it's all about Brit. We can't lose him. Come on." He drew Jamie closer, making sure to stay out of the doctor's way.

He stood, with his hand on Jamie's back as Jamie leaned down and stroked Brit's head, neck and shoulder. He talked into Brit's ear, softly, teasing and promising all kinds of dog dreams fulfilled if he would just hang on. Grant was tired, but he wouldn't have moved for anything. He supported Jamie and Brit.

Jamie's cell phone rang, making them all jump. Grant reached into Jamie's pocket and grabbed it, handing it over to Jamie.

"Yeah?" Jamie muttered then jerked straight up. "No shit! Can you bring it or part of it? I know the police will need to see it, but the doc needs to test it." He listened a second then said, "Thanks, man."

Jamie looked from Grant to the doctor and said, fury in his voice, "They found a wrapper with part of the hamburger left in it. It smells funny, they said. Tony's having Jim bring it here. The police can come here and get it. Grant," he turned to look at Grant with anguish in his eyes as he began to shake again, "he tried to kill Brit."

"We'll catch him...and he'll pay. Right now, focus on Brit. I'll go wait for Jim and bring the stuff back here, okay?"

Jamie took a second to really look at Grant, realisation of all that Grant was doing for him in his eyes, "Thanks so much."

"It's okay. I love him, too. You stay with Brit now. I'll be right back."

A couple of hours later, things were about the same. Jim had brought the wrapper and the little bit of meat left in it, and the doctor had tested it, shaking his head sadly. He'd told them it was up to Brit now. He'd cleaned him out as much as he could and was giving Brit the right kinds of medicines to counteract the poison.

The police had been by, and the doctor had told them that there was no doubt this was an attempt to kill Brit. There was enough poison on the little bit of meat left to have done it, and Brit had evidently eaten more than that.

Jamie and Grant were in shock. Right now the doctor had gone into his office to look something up. Brit's breathing was laboured, and he twitched from time to time. Once in a while, he would groan as a cramp grabbed him and moved through his body. Every time he did that, Jamie would stiffen as if the cramp hurt him, too. Grant was sure it was.

They'd brought in a couple chairs from the waiting room so they could sit in the room with Brit. Time had no meaning as they sat together, holding hands, each with the a hand on Brit. They softly stroked him, taking turns talking to him, promising crazy things if he would just get better.

Jamie leaned over and put his head on Grant's shoulder for a moment.

"I'm so tired, Grant, and so scared," he finally admitted. He hadn't said anything before about his fear, but the fatigue seemed to free him to speak from his heart.

"I know, baby. Me, too. Hang in there a little longer. I know he'll make it. He loves you so much. He'll fight to hold on." Grant tried his best to find the right thing to say.

"I don't know if it's right to want him to keep on hurting like this. He hurts so much. I can feel the tremors and cramps, and I just want him to...to not hurt anymore." Jamie rolled his forehead against the point of Grant's shoulder.

"I do, too, Jamie, but don't you give up on him. He's a strong, healthy animal. Don't let him hear you talk like that." Grant had a hard time saying that to Jamie when he felt the same way, but he felt it was important for Brit to hear their voices and to hear good things.

Jamie sat up straight and turned to look at Grant.

"You're right...again. I'm being a wimp and thinking of myself, not Brit. I wouldn't have made it through this without you, Grant. No, don't say anything. You know it. You've held us both together. Thank you so much."

"I'd do anything for you, haven't you figured that out yet?" Grant said, squeezing Jamie's hand.

"You're mine," Jamie whispered, just as Brit made a sound, and he turned back to the table. "Grant, does he look different to you?" he asked, hopefully. Grant was afraid to look. But he did and Brit did seem to be breathing a little easier. Was it possible?

"Doc Kev? Come quick, I think there's something going on with Brit," Jamie yelled into the open office doorway. Kevin came in, eagerly, and moved to the table. He smiled.

"Hey, he looks better. His breathing's a little easier. Let's have a look," he said, and set about checking Brit. He stood back, hooking the stethoscope around his neck.

"I think if he comes through, it will be a case of cure through love. There is no good reason for him to come through this. It's gonna be a long night. I'll be up with him if you all want to go home and get some rest, but something tells me that's not going to happen." Kevin looked from one to the other of them.

"Not a chance," Jamie said. "Do you really think he'll pull out of this?"

"I wouldn't have given a fig for his chances at first, but I've seen miracles happen. If he makes it, you can call it that." Kevin looked from one to the other of them and suggested, "Why don't you all go get something to eat while I check out a few things? I'll let you stay with him tonight. I don't usually let owners do that, but with Brit and his training, it's a special case. Besides, if what I think is true, he needs you here to get better."

"Then..." Jamie started, but the vet raised his hand to stop him.

"But," he started, pointing at Jamie, "you need to take a break. You and Grant go, get out a little while, come back, and you'll feel better. You need to let off a little steam." He looked at Grant, who nodded, then finished, "Grant can take care of you a little longer. Go out and regroup. I'll lock up after you. You call when you're coming back in. Give me about an hour or so, then come back, okay?"

"Are you sure it's okay to leave him?" Jamie indicated Brit, lying on the table so still, so different from the way they were used to seeing him.

"I'll take care of him, I promise. Go on, now."

Jamie turned to Grant, his brows rising.

"Come on, we'll find an all-night place, grab some food, and maybe check with Officer Johnson. He should still be on duty. We probably should go by the house before we come back, too." Grant encouraged Jamie to head out like the doctor suggested.

"Okay, thanks Kevin. We'll be back." Jamie gave Brit one more head rub and then turned to Grant. He put his arm around Grant's waist, and they leaned on each other as they walked out to the car.

Jamie went with Grant to his side and helped him get settled. He probably figured it was time for him to start taking care of Grant instead of the other way around. After getting into his seat, he looked over at Grant.

"Are you doing okay? It's been a hard night, and I've leaned on you a lot," he asked, reaching over to touch the back of Grant's neck. "Man, you just took over and got things done. Thanks for that. I just lost it, didn't I?" Jamie asked, looking amazed now that he had time to think back over the night. "I was useless," he mused.

"No, you were in shock. Man, whatever that was hit Brit hard and fast. There wasn't time for much of a reaction."

"Yeah, but you were strong. You're my big strong guy, aren't you?" Jamie said, squeezing Grant's neck.

"Yes. I am." Grant moved his neck back, pressing into Jamie's hand, turning to look at Jamie. "Let's go. We need to get a lot done and get back to Brit."

They decided to run by the house first, check on things there, call the police from the car then stop for something to eat on the way back to the vet's office. They talked about getting something for Kevin, too.

Both were surprised to find over half the people from the party still there when they pulled up. Tony met them at the door, ushering them into the living room where friends sat around talking quietly. They all asked about Brit. Jamie told them what was going on and that they were on their way back. He told them Brit nearly died and still could. He thanked Tony and Jim for their help earlier and told them all how much it meant that they'd stayed to hear about Brit.

"We were all worried about Brit, Jamie, but we stayed for you and Grant," Tony said, while others nodded. They all came by giving him hugs or back slaps on their way out. Tony told them about his talk with Officer Johnson.

They'd found the wrapper just at the outside of the gate. Donnie must have just reached in with the food and dropped it for some reason. No one doubted it was him, but it wouldn't matter if they couldn't find him. Grant watched as Jamie's shoulders dropped. He was clearly thinking about Donnie and the things he was capable of doing. It *was* getting a little too freaky.

Gant figured if Jamie ever got his hands on the creep...well, he just better never.

The guys had cleaned up everything, washed dishes, and closed everything down. There wasn't anything Jamie and Grant had to do. After thanking Tony again, they closed the door on the last of their friends. It was silent for a moment, too silent.

Grant said, "Come with me?"

"What? We've got to get..."

"Just for ten minutes. I'll even set the timer from the kitchen. Please, just ten minutes," Grant pleaded. Jamie let Grant lead him into the bedroom, sat down when Grant pushed him a little and scooted over so Grant could join him.

As soon as they were both lying down, Grant turned and opened his arms. Jamie lost it then. He started to shake and fought sobs as Grant pulled him in and rocked him from side to side. Jamie kept sucking in air, trying not to give in to the tears.

"Stop it! Just stop it," Grant said, squeezing him tighter. "Cry. Just cry, Jamie. You've got to get it out. You're wound so tight. I know how you feel, baby. Just let it go." He put his hand on the back of Jamie's head and held it to his shoulder, giving him a loving place to hide. "You've been holding in the fear, anger, pain, and questions. You're hungry, tired, scared, and you've held it in too long."

He tightened his arms as Jamie gave in, and he heard one sob, then Jamie's shoulders began to shake as tears rolled into Grant's neck. He was pleased Jamie was finally letting go of some of the terrible tension he'd been holding inside him. He stroked his hands over Jamie's head, neck, shoulders and back. He rocked him and crooned to him, telling him what a good daddy he was and how much Brit loved him, what a good time they'd have when he came home and how many ways they'd find to spoil him. He checked his watch as Jamie gave a great sigh and settled onto Grant, a dead weight.

He decided they could grab something to take with them to eat. Jamie needed a few minutes rest. He held him while he slept for about twenty minutes.

"Hey, Jamie, wake up, babe. It's time to go back and see about Brit," he whispered into Jamie's ear, right beside his head. Jamie jerked awake against him, raising his head and looking lost.

"Hey, I'm glad you got a little snooze. It's time to go back now. You hit the bathroom, and I'll make us a couple of sandwiches to eat on the way. I'll make one for Kevin, too. And I'll bring a whole bag of nacho chips, okay?" he teased, pushing against Jamie to get him to get moving.

"No."

"No?" Grant was confused. No, what?

"You're right. It's time to go back…for Brit. But first, I'm taking a minute for something equally important." With that, he dropped his mouth over Grant's, and it was like a match to tinder.

All the emotions they'd held in all night suddenly found an outlet. Their lips were mashed, their teeth clicked together and their tongues danced, stroking and gliding over each other. Jamie groaned and Grant answered in kind. Their bodies strained against each other as they grasped each other and held the kiss as long as they could without going up in flames.

"God, Jamie…" Grant started.

"I'm sorry…I…"

"No, no, not sorry. Just…whew! I think we need to see if I can't get that release we talked about, huh?" he turned red as he put the question to Jamie.

"Yeah, I think it should be fine, but check okay? Now, let's go see about Brit. Oh…thanks for before, I'm a little embarrassed at losing it all over you," Jamie said, He rolled off the bed and stood to help Grant up.

"No problem, Jamie. Where better, huh? Anything you need." Grant watched Jamie head into the bathroom before he headed for the kitchen to get things for them to take back with them. He had no idea when they'd be back.

Jamie called and talked to Officer Johnson on their way back to the vet's office. Grant called and let Kevin know they'd be there in minutes. He asked about Brit. He kept the news to himself and had a hard time not smiling and giving it away. Jamie was so busy listening to the officer he didn't catch on to what Grant was doing.

They got to the office and Grant grabbed his crutch and the bag with their sandwiches, cold drinks and chips. He'd even thrown in a few of another of Jamie's guilty pleasures, Little Debbie Swiss Cake Rolls. The man could eat his weight in them. Grant liked Nutty Bars himself, from the freezer. He hurried to catch up and go in with Jamie. He wanted to see his face when he saw Brit.

Kevin met them and told Jamie that he thought Brit might pull through. It would still be a long night, though. He opened the door to the room where Brit lay on the table.

"Brit!" Jamie said, his eyes going wide as he rushed over. Brit's tail gave a little thump against the table, and his eyes were open, looking at Jamie. They were a little glazed-looking, but he was awake.

Grant put down his bag down on one of the chairs and went over to the table where Jamie bent over, kissing the top of Brit's head and rubbing his shoulder.

"Oh, I knew you could do it, boy. I told you. You're my Whistlebritches, aren't you? Just look at you," he sniffed once and looked up at Kevin.

"Is he going to be okay, really?" There was such hope in Jamie's question.

"There's a good chance now. He woke up a few minutes ago. He's a little too sick to thrash around, but I could tell he wanted to get up and find you. You did it, Jamie. I didn't think he would come out of it," Kevin admitted now that the crisis seemed over.

Grant pulled out the food they'd brought for Kevin and listened as he told Jamie all about what he'd done for Brit. It was over his head, but he didn't care. As long as Brit would be all right and Jamie would be happy, it was all good. He set the sack back into the chair and stepped over to Jamie, putting his arms around him.

"It's great, huh?" he said, hugging Jamie, not caring that Kevin was right there. Kevin looked at the two of them and laughed.

"I'm going to take this in my office and grab a few minutes to eat and write this up. You all make yourselves comfortable out here. Call me if there's any change." He headed into the office and closed the door most of the way.

Jamie turned and took Grant fully into his arms and just picked him up. Grant gasped then chuckled, impressed. Not many people could pick up someone who was as big as he was. He laughed down at Jamie, happiness creeping in and pushing out the anger and fear that had lived inside him all night.

"Put me down, you goof," he said, his arms around Jamie's neck.

"Your goof," Jamie said, smiling up at him.

Grant looked down at him, holding his gaze as he slid back down to the floor, still tight against Jamie.

"My goof. Yes, mine," Grant said, mimicking their earlier exchange.

They both turned when Brit whimpered. He was jealous. It looked like he wanted some of that lovin' for himself. They both gave it. He was rubbed and kissed and talked to for a long time. He eventually closed his eyes and they moved to the chairs.

Grant got their picnic supper together, and Jamie's eyes lit up when he saw what all Grant had brought.

"I thought you needed a special treat after the night you've had."

"You're so good to me...for me," Jamie stated.

They ate, feeding each other now and then, reaching up every once in a while to touch the sleeping Brit. He was so special to both of them.

Kevin came back in eventually and checked on Brit. As the sun came up he told them, "I think Brit's going to be fine. He made it through the worst of it. His vitals are much better. Why don't you all go home and get some real rest."

"Are you sure...?" Jamie got no further.

"Look, I'll be keeping Brit for a couple of days to make sure he's clear of the poison. You all can come back and visit, but he's going to sleep a lot. It'll be good for him. Right now, I think it'd be good for you two, as well."

Chapter Seven

It was a couple of very tired, happy boys who headed home early that Sunday morning. They fell into bed and were asleep before they could even kiss each other goodnight...or good morning. Both slept hard for several hours, getting up in the early afternoon. They called Doc Kev and were told that Brit was improving, but he was sleeping and they didn't need to come in. He suggested they come by about six or seven for a short visit.

They walked around the house, nibbled on some fruit and dry cereal in the kitchen, walked out onto the patio.

Jamie sighed deeply. "I feel kinda lost. I don't have any studying to do, and you don't need any more exercise now. I miss Brit."

Finally, Grant tried to say what he'd been thinking about for the last hour or so.

"Can we...will you...I mean..." He blushed.

"Oh, this must be about sex if you can't even say it," Jamie teased, walking right up to Grant and taking him into his arms. "I love the way you blush and stammer, then when we're in bed, you'll try anything."

"Shut up. Don't laugh at me, goof. I want…"

"You want what? Say it," Jamie prodded, running his forefinger down the side of Grant's face, causing him to shiver.

"I want to take a shower with you. I want you. I want us to go to bed and make each other happy." Grant leaned back in Jamie's arms, knowing he would be held safely. "We don't need to talk to anyone about it. You know I'm not going to hurt myself just making love." He looked into Jamie's eyes, his clear and bright. "I'm not going to be swinging from the ceiling fan, but we don't have to wait any longer. I want to know what it feels like to have you inside me, taking me, making me yours." His cheeks were red after the honesty of his desire was vocalised. "You can find a way that won't mess up anything. I'm tired of waiting."

Jamie hugged him tight, crossing both arms around his neck and pulling him in for a full body hug. Grant snuggled right in, arms grasped around Jamie's waist, clasping him just as tight.

"Me, too," Jamie whispered. "Been wanting you so long…so long." He pushed his groin against Grant's letting him see how much. The evidence of Grant's reciprocal need was right there. They both groaned as they moved against each other.

"That feels so good."

"Mmm, I think we can come up with a way that won't cause a problem for your health and wellbeing,"

Jamie teased, moving his weight from foot to foot, rocking them back and forth.

"Right now my health and wellbeing would be improved if we could take this to the bedroom and you show me what you're talking about. We've got all afternoon." Grant turned his head and licked a swipe up Jamie's throat to that spot behind his ear that always made him shiver. Score! He chuckled, clearly pleased at his teasing and the results.

Jamie laughed with him as they both turned and headed for the bedroom. Growing excitement kept them both quiet as they reached the room and headed for the shower.

"Are you...?" Jamie started and Grant interrupted him.

"Don't you even ask if I'm sure or if I'm ready. I'm so sure and so far past ready it's not even funny. Just don't make me wait any longer," Grant pleaded, moving his hand over Jamie's chest and stomach.

"You got it," Jamie said, huskily, leaning to take Grant's mouth in a voracious kiss. It seemed like only seconds before they were both naked and stepping into the shower stall. Jamie got the water going just right for what he planned. He didn't want a hard spray and a hurried washing. He wanted to play and push a little and build up the tension and need. He turned and pulled Grant to him under the soft warm mist.

He put both hands onto the top of Grant's head and moved them over him sliding down the back of his neck and shoulders. He loved the way Grant looked with the water collecting on his lashes then rolling down his cheeks. He leaned in and put his lips to

Grant's forehead, following it down beside his eye and down to his cheek. He nibbled the corner of Grant's mouth, teasing it with his tongue, smiling as Grant opened for him. Tongues met and teased, sipping water and curling together.

Jamie hummed as Grant's hands came up to cup his face, holding him still for Grant's mouth to take over the kiss. He took great delight in the way Grant took control, and soon, they were crushed together, moaning into each other's mouths. They stood for a long time just like that, Grant's hands keeping Jamie right where he wanted him, Jamie's moving on Grant's shoulders, holding tight. Neither of them wanted to budge an inch from where they were.

Finally Jamie pulled back a little and looked at a dazed Grant. "Turn around and hold onto the wall for me," he requested. Grant turned without question and put both hands onto the wall. He looked over his shoulder at Jamie and the anticipation in his eyes made Jamie melt right there.

Jamie got the soap, lathered his hands and moved from Grant's neck to his heels, paying close and tender attention to the crease between his buttocks. When he was finished he was kneeling on the floor of the shower, face level with Grant's beautiful backside.

"Hang on, baby. This is a new one for you," Jamie said, reaching up and spreading Grant's cheeks. Grant slipped his feet a little further apart to make it easier for Jamie to get to him. He pushed back a little, too, making it clear that he was ready for what Jamie had in mind for him.

Jamie leaned in and put his mouth to the sensitive area around Grant's virgin hole. He had caressed this area a few times, fleetingly, but they'd not done too much, knowing they couldn't follow through. Today, they would be able to go there, at last. Grant jumped and gasped, then settled, waiting for more.

Jamie held him firmly apart and let his tongue come into play, moving it around and around the tight circle. He pushed it inside and felt Grant clench it tight. He kept on, again and again, getting a little further each time. Grant was gasping, sighing, moaning, and keening as he absorbed the wonderful sensations. Soon Jamie had a hard time holding Grant still. He moved his thumbs close to where his tongue disappeared inside and massaged the tight skin around the area. Grant flexed the muscles in his ass, making it hard as rock against Jamie's fingers that were spread over it. Jamie felt the tremors that shook Grant as he got closer and closer to climax.

Jamie decided to end it for him. He slid out his tongue and replaced it with the finger of one hand. The other hand slid down and skated over the tight, drawn up balls and grasped the hard cock that was curved up and touching Grant's stomach. He didn't have to spend a lot of time there. He circled it, squeezed it, and held on while Grant shot hard. Grant squeezed Jamie's finger inside him and filled his other hand with hot cum. Jamie leaned in and kissed the cheek closest to him before easing his finger out and pulling back a little.

Jamie looked up as Grant turned around, holding onto the wall for support, looking dazed and confused for a few seconds. When Grant looked down at Jamie, his eyes opened wide and a smile split his face. He reached down and helped Jamie to stand, taking him right into his arms and holding on. Jamie groaned as Grant rubbed himself against Jamie's body, snuggling and sighing.

"Don't let me go. I may not be able to stand on my own," he said, kissing Jamie over and over, with quick, happy kisses.

"Wasn't planning to," Jamie teased him back. "Like that, huh?"

"Get me out of here. I can't kneel on this knee yet, and I really think I'd like to do something about this," he said, reaching down and taking hold of Jamie's hard cock.

Jamie thought Grant had been talking about going to the bed, but as soon as they were out of the shower he drew Jamie over to the toilet, put the top down, sat down, and pulled Jamie to him. He put one hand on Jamie's hip and the other around his cock, drawing it forward to his lips. He opened wide and took as much as he could into his mouth then closed around it and sucked in, his cheeks pulling tight.

Jamie dropped back his head and put both hands on Grant's head. He held on, and it wasn't long at all before he had to pull out and Grant took him into his hand and finished him off. He gasped and groaned as he shot long and hard into Grant's hand, getting some on his chest. Grant just looked up at him and smiled. He stood up again and pulled him back into the shower, starting it and putting Jamie under the spray. This time it was just a quick in and out, soap and wash, and done.

They stood and just looked at each other, grinning like the goofs they were, as they took a few seconds to dry each other off, quickly and efficiently. Soon they were back in the bedroom and scooting onto the bed together.

Jamie reached over to the bedside table for the lube and condoms. They'd already had 'the talk' much earlier in their relationship. They both knew they were clean and clear, but decided to take great care with each other. Maybe someday, after they'd been together long enough to know they'd be exclusive, they might go bare, but right now, safety was the word.

"I'm ridiculously nervous," Grant said, watching Jamie closely.

"Don't be. I've got you," Jamie said, and that was all it took.

"Oh, I'm not worried about me. I know you'll take good care of me. I just want to take good care of you, too, ya know?" Grant asked, looking at Jamie like he really thought there might be a way he could mess this up.

"After that performance in there, you're worried about making me happy?"

"What? It was just a blow job. You…"

Jamie interrupted him. "Did it make you happy?"

"Huh?"

"Did giving me a blow job make you happy?" Jamie knew what he was doing.

Grant thought about it. "Yes, it *did* make me happy."

"Why?" Jamie had one more question.

"Why? Because it made you feel good, made you happy…" Finally, it seemed to dawn on Grant what Jamie was trying to get across to him. Anything that made Jamie feel good would make Grant feel good and vice versa. There wasn't anything to worry about because any way they touched each other was good and brought them both joy.

"Okay. Sometimes I'm amazed at my own stupidity. You are so right. There's nothing to be nervous about because with us, it's all good. Yeah?" Grant watched Jamie nod and smile as he finally got it.

"It's okay, baby. A lot of people fall into that. They hear about something and build it up until it's something that has to be perfect. That's not the way." Jamie reached out and took Grant's hand in his, linking their fingers. "It just has to be us, touching, feeling, and doing as much as we want, as our bodies will let us." Jamie stretched out and kept talking, still holding Grant's hand in his. "But all of it's together and for each other. Along the way there may be something one of us doesn't particularly like. In that case, we say it, and that makes it right for us. Don't ever endure something you're uncomfortable with because you think it's something I want." He squeezed Grant's fingers, stressing the point. "That would make me unhappy, because if it's not making you happy then I won't feel good about it. Same goes, both ways. This is a lot of talk and not enough do, but it's good that we understand all this now. You okay with all this?"

"I'm fine with it. I agree with everything you said. We'll learn together. I can tell you I'd never be comfortable with any kind of bondage thing or tying me up or stuff like that. Freaks me out to think of it," Grant admitted.

"Cool, never appealed to me, either. Never did it, never wanted to, so we're off to a good start. Now, tell me something you *have* thought about that you'd like to try…not necessarily today. Today will be very easy and straightforward. But, come on, share a fantasy with me."

"Hell, the only fantasies I've had have starred you, but I'll play. Hmmm…" He pretended to think about it, then said, "I like it that this bed is kind of high. I've thought about you bending me over it and taking me that way."

Jamie's eyes got big, and he smiled. "Well, hello. Good one, and one I can promise to fulfil. As a matter of fact, that should be one that wouldn't hurt your injuries at all so count on that happening really soon." Jamie winked at Grant.

"I'd love to know some of yours," Grant said. "Especially ones about me."

"Baby, they've all been about you since I first met you," Jamie said, leaning over to lick across Grant's lips. "Even before I found out you wouldn't knock me out for thinking them." He smiled as Grant chuckled.

"So," Grant drawled, stretching the word out. "Give. Fantasy, you and me…doing what?"

"Hmm, well, there's the one where you do to me what I did to you in there," he said, pointing to the bathroom.

"Okay, rimming. I think I'd like to do that for you," Grant said. "Anything else?"

"As I said before, too much talk, not enough do." Jamie smoothed his hand down Grant's chest to his stomach, smiling as Grant sucked it in and pushed forward to get more of his touch. "Now, no more talk, lots of action. Here's what I think would work best for you right now."

He had Grant stretch out onto his left side with his right knee bent forward. He placed a pillow under the knee, thus giving the knee a place to rest. This way the hip would not be taxed. Another plus was that it made it easy to get to Grant without putting weight onto him at all.

Jamie massaged down Grant's back, pressing in and relaxing the muscles. He leaned in to whisper into his ear. "Soon we'll be able to do this facing each other, which is how I prefer it. I want to see your eyes when I slide into that sweet, hot hole. I'll wait for that. This is safer for you. I'll be easy with you. Don't worry."

"Jamie, I'm not worried, really. I want you. I want this," Grant assured him, turning his head to look at Jamie over his shoulder. Jamie reached up and took his mouth in a kiss that rocked them both. He pushed his tongue in and began a back and forth motion that had them both breathing hard and straining to be closer. Jamie had to pull back and get back to what he was doing.

He took the lube, getting his fingers liberally coated. He reached down and spread it along Grant's crack. Grant jumped because it was cold but then pushed back towards Jamie, letting him know it was what he wanted. Jamie was lying close behind Grant, resting on one elbow, using his other to caress the tender skin around Grant's tight hole.

Jamie leaned and kissed the shoulder near him, whispering to Grant about how hot he was, how much he wanted him, and how good he would make it for him. He told him what he would do before he did it, making sure it wasn't a jolt or unwelcome.

"I'm going to put one finger inside you now, slow and gentle, mmmhmm, you like that, don't you? Yes, that's my guy. Show me how much."

Grant moved for him, pushing back against the finger that was still inching inward. He moved it back out all the way, then eased it back in, noting how Grant shivered each time the digit breached the tight circle. He began to move it in and out, making sure it was still liberally coated. He added more lube then told Grant he was going to add another finger and to let him know if it was okay.

Jamie kept up his movements and the continual words, turning Grant into a quivering mass of need. He bent his head to Grant's neck, kissing and nibbling as he kept up the soft action below. Finally, when he had been moving steadily in and out with three fingers, Jamie deemed Grant ready to accept him inside.

"Okay, I think you're ready for the real thing, now, aren't you?' Jamie asked, his chin resting on Grant's shoulder. Grant's face was turned to look back at him. Jamie's heart clutched at the look on Grant's face. He was flushed and his eyes were half-closed in a mixture of ecstasy and need. Jamie thought he'd never seen a sexier sight. He had to lean over and take Grant's mouth again and try to absorb some of those feelings into himself.

"Please…Jamie…please…" was all Grant could say when Jamie pulled his lips away.

"Okay," Jamie said, "I know, baby, I just had to make sure. I want this to be good for you." He had never been in the position of being someone's first before, and as if that wasn't enough pressure, it was Grant. He loved this man.

He covered and slicked himself then reached to touch Grant, letting him know it was time. He put the tip of his cock to Grant's entrance and pushed, feeling the initial resistance. Grant moaned but pushed back before Jamie could stop to see if it was in pain or pleasure. Obviously, he was taking no chances on Jamie stopping.

Jamie wasn't going to stop. Once the flared tip of his cock was inside he paused a second, letting Grant get used to having him there. It wasn't long at all before he pushed harder, steadily sliding in until he was seated all the way, his balls flush with Grant's ass. He put his arm over the top of Grant's thigh, avoiding the still tender flesh of his hip injury. He held on and began to draw back out.

"Oh, oh Jamie, that…that feels so…God, that feels like…" Grant stopped, unable to go on.

Jamie paused, looking up to see Grant's face. There were tears in his eyes. Jamie nearly pulled out and stopped completely, but Grant reached down and put his right hand on top of Jamie's, holding him there.

"Grant, baby, what is it? Am I hurting you? Do you want me to stop?" Jamie couldn't stand the thought of that. But he couldn't bear to see Grant with tears running down his face either.

"Home. It feels like home. Like I'm where I'm supposed to be, finally." Grant pulled his hand up, brushing the tears off his face. "Please, don't stop. Don't ever stop, Jamie. More. I want more. I know I sound stupid, but…"

"Shh, baby. Hush, now. I'm not stopping. Don't you worry," Jamie said, starting to move again, still slow and steady, but complete. All the way out, then all the way back in. He knew it felt good to Grant when he felt that thickness opening him up, so he made sure he did that several times before he got serious and held on to his leg and kept up a steady in and out motion.

"Home," he said, rubbing his head against Grant's shoulder. "This feels like home to you. You *are* home now, Grant. Your home is right here. I've got your home right here." Grant's wording had touched him deeply. He loved that Grant felt that way. He wanted to tell Grant that he loved him, but he wouldn't now. He didn't want it to be part of this. He wouldn't have Grant thinking it had anything to do with sex. He loved him, just loved him.

Grant rocked back against Jamie. He was obviously feeling no pain at all in any of the injuries, and he was flying, just flying on the feelings Jamie filled him with.

"More, Jamie. Just a little harder. I'm fine, really." Grant wanted to feel him really let go. He put his hand on Jamie's again and linked their fingers and pushed back with his hip, forcing Jamie deeper into him.

Jamie paid him the compliment of taking his word for it, knowing he wouldn't take a chance with his health. He rammed into him a couple of times and was thrilled when Grant shouted, "Yes!"

Jamie slid both their hands down to grasp Grant's cock and began to pump it in rhythm to his thrusts. Before long Grant was coming, hot musky fluid covering both their hands. Jamie wasn't far behind. He thrust once more into Grant and felt the tightness gathering in his balls and the burning heat of his orgasm was filling the condom.

He pulled his hand back and very carefully eased out of Grant, making sure the condom was still intact. He lay back, took a deep breath, then reached to remove it, tying it off and dropping it into the trashcan by the bed. Right now, he had to hold Grant. He took a couple of tissues and swept them over Grant, cleaning him up a little then himself. He dropped them with the condom then turned to help Grant ease down onto his back, moving the pillow and making sure he wasn't having any problems.

Jamie climbed over to the other side of Grant so he could lean over his left side and hold him. He put his weight onto his left elbow, stretching up and looking down into Grant's eyes.

"Are you okay?" he asked, quietly, watching Grant's eyes to make sure he could read the truth there.

"I'm fine. I've never been better. I know now. Jamie," Grant said, reaching out with his right hand and holding the side of Jamie's face, "you'll never know how much it meant to me, the care you took, the way you felt in me, the way it made me feel whole."

"I'm glad, baby."

Grant shook his head at himself. "I never knew I didn't feel whole before. Isn't that odd? But, somehow, when we were connected, I finally felt like I knew who I was and I felt complete. How strange that I've felt *in*complete without knowing it. I guess I'd have gone the rest of my life never knowing what was missing if I hadn't met you."

"Nah, you'd have found someone someday who turned your crank and made you realise that you were just a gay man who needed another gay man to make your life complete. I like it, though. I like being the one to make you feel this way. I hope it means you'll stay right here." Jamie meant that. He had no doubts about the two of them.

"I'll stay. I'll have to think about what I'm going to do soon, but right now, what time is it? We don't want to forget Brit...Whistlebritches...what a name!" Grant leaned over to look at the clock and saw that it was close to six.

"Wow, we've spent all afternoon...hmm, making love. But we should probably get up now," Grant said.

"Oh, no, not now. Don't you know, there's another of the joys I've been telling you about?" Jamie teased him.

"What?" Grant looked eager.

"You must cuddle after sex. It's almost required. Come on, slide that gorgeous body on top of mine and let's have a proper hug. A really wet kiss would be part of the scenario, too, by the way." Jamie laughed at the look on Grant's face. He was so handsome and bemusement looked good on him.

"I'm lucky I've got you to keep me up on all the joys and requirements," Grant teased him right back, crawling up and easing his body down on top of Jamie's. Jamie thought again how well they fit together. Both so tall and big and things just fell into place in the right ways.

He put his arms around Grant and pulled down his head for a really wet kiss. The joking stopped there, and the kiss seemed a serious expression of how they felt about each other, mutual, and very strong.

Eventually they got up, showered again quickly and dressed to go see Brit. They called and asked if Kevin needed anything as they came. As they sped down the street, Jamie looked over at Grant and said, "By the way, I don't just like to give it. I like to take it, too. So, sometime soon, I'd like to know what it feels like to have you inside me, reaming me out, taking me hard."

Grant nearly choked on his own saliva. He turned red and glanced over at Jamie, who looked calm like he hadn't just rocked Grant's world.

"Uh, sure, okay."

Jamie burst out laughing, reaching to take Grant's hand in his. "You're so funny. Blew your mind, didn't I?"

"Yeah," Grant admitted, ducking his head, then looking back at Jamie. "But, I think I'd love that, taking you, making you feel what I felt. My God, Jamie, it makes me shake, just thinking about it now."

"Oh, that's good." Jamie was pleased. "I like that."

Grant laughed at him, clearly tickled that he'd made him feel good, telling him how much he like making love with him.

They spent a happy hour with Brit who was in the kennel now. He didn't look like the old Brit. He moved slowly and seemed groggy, but he barked when he saw them and got up and came over to them. Kevin allowed him out of the big cage while they were there.

They both sat right down on the floor, and Brit was in heaven going back and forth between them for hugs, kisses, scratches, and rubs. He licked their faces and whined as they told him what a great dog he was and how much they missed him. It was a general love fest that didn't get old.

Finally, Brit looked sleepy so they urged him to return to the cage. It was a testament to how low he felt that he went in with no argument and settled down, his head on his paws and went right to sleep.

After thanking Kevin and promising to call in the morning, they left in search of food. Lunch had been skimpy, and they'd had quite an afternoon and evening. Jamie took Grant to a nice restaurant, and they splurged on a great dinner, followed by coffee and dessert. They both sat back and sighed, thoroughly happy with life and each other.

When they got back to the car there was a note on the windshield. It was just a folded piece of notebook paper. Grant saw it first and pointed it out to Jamie, who reached for it.

"Wait. Should we call the police first? You think it's from Donnie?" Grant asked, looking around.

Jamie looked around the parking lot but saw nothing out of the ordinary. He nodded and sighed, reaching for his cell. He called the police but Officer Johnson wasn't on that night. They talked to the other officer from before, the nice one, Mark Thomas. Jamie told the officer that he hadn't touched the paper yet. Since there was no one around, no imminent threat, the officer suggested Jamie take it down and read it, to make sure it wasn't just an advertisement for something local. Jamie did and held the phone away from his mouth as he cursed. He showed it to Grant.

It said, "How's Brit?"

There was a crude drawing of a dog lying down with blood coming from his mouth. Grant immediately put his arm around Jamie's waist and held on as Jamie shook, either from fury or fear.

"I tell you what, I'll bring it down to the station. You can have it, and it will be on the report. I know who wrote it. It means that Donnie's taking responsibility for this, and that he's following us."

Jamie and Grant took the note, calling Kevin on the way to make sure he was safely locked in. They made out a report and gave the letter to Officer Thomas. Of course, there was nothing to be done since no one knew where Donnie was. Jamie suggested the police follow them home, since Donnie probably would. He was half-joking and half-serious. Hell, Jamie wondered if Donnie really *was* out there waiting to follow them home, or if maybe he was already there, waiting for them.

It was a much more subdued couple who left the station and headed home. Jamie was furious at the thought that they'd been so happy when leaving the restaurant and feeling all had been right with their world and now they were smack dab back in to the middle of Donnie's game.

"Jamie?" Grant eventually said, putting his hand on Jamie's thigh as he drove. Jamie put his hand down on top of Grant's.

"Yeah?" He sounded depressed. That was so unlike the Jamie that Grant had come to know.

"Don't do this. Don't let this bastard win. He wants to blow your world apart, separate us, hurt you or me or both of us. It just makes me *mad*. I don't want to give him the satisfaction of thinking he's succeeding."

"You're right. I'm sorry. I'm just so frustrated. Why can't the police find him? He comes and goes all the time. They haven't even served him the order yet. He's like a fucking ghost." He glanced quickly over at Grant, trying to smile for him and failing miserably.

"I know, let's go home, windows down, music on, singing and laughing and hope to hell he is within hearing distance. Let's stop and kiss on the front porch and hope he sees us. Let's let him know that he can't break us down or break us apart," Grant said, his voice quivering a little with the passion of his feelings about what was happening to them.

"Damn! You're my big tough guy, aren't you? I love that. You got it, baby. Put on some Bon Jovi. How about Have a Nice Day? That's the appropriate sentiment, I do believe. We'll do just what you said, to the letter." Jamie brought Grant's hand up to his mouth to kiss the back of it before replacing it on his leg, this time up closer to his crotch. He moved it back and forth a little, smiling as Grant pressed down, obviously wanting to let Jamie know he was right there with him.

As they pulled into the driveway, they sat for a few minutes waiting for the right words to come along and they both got out singing along with it about not doing anything he didn't want to, he was gonna live his life, and if the world got in his face he'd just tell them to have a nice day. It was the song's use of the words 'Have a nice day' as a euphemism for 'Fuck you' that made it just right for the way Jamie was feeling right then.

Jamie thought it was perfect. He knew they were using it to tell Donnie to come on, he could try, but they'd still be standing in the end telling him to go to hell. Feeling strong in the heat of the moment, they followed their scenario. Stopping by the front door to embrace, Jamie planted a long kiss on Grant's eager mouth. The area was sort of hidden from the street with the way the porch hung over and the front room sort of jutted out and hid them from view. They weren't exhibitionists. Jamie figured no one else was watching, but if Donnie was indeed around, let him look. It was all for him, anyway. How dare he try to ruin their evening?

As soon as they were inside with the door closed and locked, Grant took Jamie's hand and pulled him towards the bedroom.

"You got something in mind there, big guy?" Jamie teased, hoping he did.

"I do. I've got a fantasy to fulfil. I know just what I want to do, after we take a shower together." He drew Jamie into the bathroom and started removing his shirt. "I feel like I want to wash away any lingering thoughts of Devil Donnie and just focus on us." He started on Jamie's shorts, smiling into Jamie's eyes the whole time. "Then, I've got a plan for…taking it to the rim…so to speak…" He laughed with Jamie at the poor play on words. But Jamie seemed eager to get with the plan.

Grant deviated from his plan just a little. They showered together, enjoying the water and each other, but they didn't linger there. As soon as they were both dried off, Grant took Jamie's hand and led him into the bedroom. Jamie might have assumed they were headed for the bed, but Grant stopped right inside the door and pushed him up against the wall. Jamie's eyes widened as he waited to see just what Grant had planned for him.

Grant stepped up to Jamie but stopped just when their bodies were barely brushing against each other. He silently pushed on Jamie's shoulders, indicating that he wanted him to stay back against the wall. Jamie nodded and waited, his senses heightened by the very difference in what they were doing. They weren't talking, laughing, kissing, or any of the other things they usually did after a shower...and before bed.

Standing so very close to Jamie, Grant took a visual tour, not missing a point. He let his eyes show how pleased he was with what he saw. Grant leaned a little towards Jamie, putting his face close to Jamie's neck and breathing in. He let a sigh escape, letting Jamie know he liked the way he smelled. Jamie shivered at this small thing, this evidence that his scent turned Grant on. They both stood still, just breathing in and out, the tempo increasing as their anticipation mounted. Finally, Grant moved his head a little, putting his tongue out and touching the corner of Jamie's shoulder, just a taste. He gave a very quiet hum, again letting Jamie know how much he liked it.

Grant didn't know where he got the idea. He was just following his heart and his instincts. He could tell Jamie enjoyed what he was doing, so he continued. His fingers came into play, lightly touching Jamie's chest, here, there, around. A smile lit his face as Jamie sucked in his stomach when Grant's fingers traced a line straight from the centre of his collarbone down past his navel. The finger stopped just short of touching the hard erection just below. Jamie began to shiver, a full body shiver. It was obvious he was having a hard time being still but was also dying to see what Grant was going to do next.

Grant leaned down a little and touched the tip of his tongue to the hard point of Jamie's left nipple. He closed his eyes and moved over to the other one, just barely touching it but getting a loud moan from Jamie all the same. It was good, he thought, what he was doing. Without thinking about it as such, he worshipped Jamie's body, giving it the honour he felt it was due. He stepped back a little, looked Jamie up and down, then leaned in again to touch his tongue to the crease where his arm met his torso, right in front of his armpit. Jamie gasped. Who knew? Grant pulled back and did the same to the other side. Jamie was ready for it this time, not gasping but pushing forward a little to get more of the touch.

Pulling back, Grant looked into Jamie's eyes. They almost glowed with need and interest. He still stood with his back against the wall, but Grant felt him straining to get closer, feel more. He put his hands on the wall on either side of Jamie, leaned down, trailing his tongue, very lightly down Jamie's stomach. Jamie shuddered. Grant smiled to himself. He eased a little to the side, moving his lips, oh so gently, around to Jamie's ribs. Jamie raised his arms, allowing Grant access to him, willing to accept anything Grant wanted to do.

Grant really hadn't planned all this, but it was going so well, he didn't want to stop. He gave some attention to Jamie's other side, then pulled back and made a twirling motion with his finger. He wanted Jamie facing the wall. Jamie, being no fool, turned and obeyed Grant's silent demand. Grant gave Jamie's shoulders, spine, ribs, and the small of his back the same light, airy attention.

He didn't apply a lot of pressure, just a touch, just a tribute to all of Jamie, showing his affection for all of the man. This time he went below the waist. He still couldn't kneel so he stood back and bent from the waist so he could spend a little time on Jamie's tight, hard butt. He touched the crease, easing his finger down from top to bottom then spread Jamie's cheeks with his hands, and for just a second, he touched his tongue to Jamie's tight hole. This time Jamie made some noise.

"Grant! God, you're killin' me," Jamie said, but he didn't move or turn. He stood still and waited to see what Grant would do next. Grant stood up straight, moved forward, and pressed the whole of his body against Jamie's. His cock rested in the small of Jamie's back. He moved his hips against Jamie's and heard a sob from his lover. He put his hands on Jamie's shoulders and turned him around, keeping full contact with him as he did.

Jamie clearly couldn't take it anymore. He put his arms around Grant's shoulders and leaned to take Grant's mouth with his. It wasn't gentle. He swept in and devoured Grant's lips, pushed his tongue in and began a thrusting motion that had both of them sucking in air. Finally, they had to stop and get a good deep breath.

"Grant...baby..." Jamie said, but stopped, as in unsure what he was going to say. Grant looked at him and smiled, a big, wide, happy smile. Then Jamie knew what to say. "Fuck me, suck me, rim me, finger me, *something*. Just take me. I'm about to lose it. You are the sexiest thing I've ever known." Jamie shook from head to toe as he begged. "Don't leave me like this."

"Come on over here. I'm not going to leave you like that. How about leaning over the bed right here for me?" He drew Jamie to the bed, and gave him a gentle push, so he was bent over the side of the bed, his ass in the air. "I'm going to start with the rimming I promised you, then, I'm going to put my cock right where you want it most. You ready for that?" Grant leaned down and put a quick kiss on Jamie's right cheek.

"Mmm….Mmm," Jamie said. Grant took that for a yes. He reached for a pillow and urged Jamie to rise up. He put the pillow right at the edge of the bed so Jamie had a softer place to rest that part of his body that was soon to be slammed a bit.

Grant moved away for a moment, going into the bathroom and retrieving a stool that he brought over to the bedside. He sat, thus resting his hip and his ankle but putting him in perfect position for the task at hand. It might have looked a little odd, but that wasn't a problem. Making his man happy was the goal here.

He bent and touched the tip of his tongue to the top of Jamie's crack and dragged it backwards down to the base of his balls. He held Jamie wide open for him to pleasure. He revelled in Jamie's moans and shivers, and he reversed his route then settled in for a long and thorough investigation of the joys of rimming someone he loved. The pleasure gained from making him sigh and squirm and plead. The knowledge that he gave the ultimate intense feelings. Having had his own personal lesson he didn't miss a trick, moving his tongue agilely over the area then pointing it and thrusting it inside. He knew Jamie loved it, because the man was far from quiet.

"Jesus, Grant…oh…there…yeah…good." A couple of deep breaths, then, "Oh yeah, please, more, Grant, yeah…oh…" The noises kept coming, and they kept Grant working to get more and more of the happy sounds, evidence of the good job he did. He moved his head back and watched as he placed his index finger into the well-lubricated hole. Just that little bit bigger in size and Jamie was squirming and moaning again.

Grant reached for the lube and greased his fingers and set about preparing Jamie for the grand finale. His own cock was bumping his belly leaving trails of pre-cum, evidence of his own excitement. He took his time and gradually got up to three fingers inside Jamie. Jamie came up off the bed and rested on his elbows, pushing back and essentially fucking himself on Grant's fingers.

"Sexy…sexy man. More, Grant, harder now. I want your cock in me. Please, hard as you can." Jamie could barely get the words out as he heaved for breath. "You've got me wound so tight I'm gonna explode. Fuck! I want you," he ended as Grant removed his fingers at last and reached for the condom that was handy. He stood and pushed the stool out of the way. In a matter of seconds, he had himself ready for entry, and God knew Jamie was ready.

Grant was so intent upon making this good for Jamie that he didn't pause to be worried about how he was doing or if there was something in particular he should do. He did what came naturally. He eased in, taking great care, knowing that it had been a while for Jamie. Jamie groaned from deep in his throat as Grant's cock slid slowly and steadily inside. Grant didn't stop until his abdomen was pressed tightly to Jamie's tight buttocks. He leaned over, laying his body down onto Jamie's back. He reached down and got hold of Jamie's hands and fit his over the top of them, tangling their fingers and spread both sets of arms straight out to the sides. He planted his feet right beside Jamie's so that his legs followed Jamie's. They fit together perfectly.

Uniting. Fusing. Coupling. Melding. Merging. Grant and Jamie were as close as they could be. Grant enclosed Jamie in his embrace and held still inside him, awed by the feeling of being one with him. His face was pressed against Jamie's and he whispered his joy to his lover.

"I am part of you, Jamie. We are one unit, connected in a way I've only dreamed of before." He paused a moment, taking a deep breath, trying to find words for how he felt. "I knew the mechanics of sex, but I didn't know how I'd feel when I was inside the person that...that I have such strong feelings for." Turning his head a bit, he pressed his lips to the spot right in front of Jamie's ear and held them there. "It's incredible. Thank you."

He drew his lips to Jamie's neck and back to his shoulder. He removed them as he straightened and began to ease back out of Jamie. *Oh*...that was incredible, indeed. He began to move back and forth, easily. This way he could move freely, putting no strain on any of his injuries.

He watched Jamie as he moved in a continuous rhythm, in and out. Sometimes he held onto Jamie's hips and thrust hard into him several times, loving the shout he heard each time he did. He would return to the slow steady thrusts that he felt like he could keep up forever. He'd have thought that the first time he did this he'd go off like a sparkler. He had no idea why he was able to continue, but he wasn't going to spend time on that. Jamie was beginning to show signs of being close to coming for him.

"Grant, I'm gonna...please...touch me..." Jamie said, brokenly.

Grant complied with his wishes and reached down to take him in hand and with a few strong strokes he collected a handful of hot cum and heard Jamie groan hard. He gave Jamie a couple of minutes to come down then he held onto his hips again and rammed hard a few times, feeling the cum seem to boil up from the base of his balls and stream out into the condom. He held tight and just pushed into Jamie again and again, until he couldn't stand up any more. He fell on top of Jamie, this time in exhaustion

How long they lay like that, they neither knew nor cared. Finally, though, Grant had to move to ease the muscles in his back and hips. He pushed himself up and carefully eased out of Jamie, taking great care with the condom. He tied it off and carefully moved back, his legs a little weak. He grinned, glancing back at Jamie who was still ass up over the side of the bed. He'd wasted him.

He headed to the bathroom and disposed of the condom and got a washcloth, cleaned himself up then wrung more hot water out of it. Walking up behind

Jamie, he brought the cloth up and smoothed it gently over him, not missing a spot that needed his attention. He reached down and took hold of one of Jamie's hands, exerting pressure to pull him up. Jamie looked like he'd been melted. His eyes were half open, his arms seemed heavy, and he stumbled a little as he stood by Grant. He looked into Grant's eyes and tried to say something that made sense.

"There are no words," he began huskily. "None." Jamie watched Grant fold the cloth into a small tight square and toss it into the bathroom before turning to him.

"I've got some words for you," Grant said, looking deeply into Jamie's sweet hot eyes. "I will tell you now, standing here, apart...well, slightly apart, that I love you." He put his hands out to cup the side of Jamie's face and held it still for him to lean over and place a soft kiss on Jamie's lips. "I love you, Jamie Taylor, like I never thought it was possible to love." Jamie reached for him, but Grant put one hand on his chest to hold him back for just a few moments.

"I admire you. I love your manner with people, your LOLs and your other patients. I love your dog and your deep love for him. I love your strength. I love your self-confidence. I love your body—oh God, I love your body." Evidently he still had the ability to blush. "I have known for a little while, but it has been growing since I met you. I felt an instant connection with you. Thank you...just for being you...and for being with me." Grant put his head down on Jamie's shoulder and wrapped his arms around him.

Jamie's arms came up to enfold Grant against him, and he gave a soft little chuckle. Supreme happiness just had to be released.

"I've known I'm in love with you for a good while," Jamie revealed. "At first, I didn't want to scare you away, then I didn't want you to think it was only physical, so I held back when we were doing anything that led up to today and tonight. I love you so much, Grant Stevens. You have become my world…and I don't see that changing. Thank you for the same things…for being you…and for being with me." Jamie put his own head down on Grant's shoulder, and they stood there, clasped together, both clearly thrilled beyond measure at being able to voice their feelings at last.

"Come to bed, lover mine," Jamie said, turning them and getting them settled on the bed, under the sheets, cuddled tightly together.

"Ah, the cuddle after sex rule," Grant teased. "I like it."

"Goof," Jamie said, sweeping his hands over Grant's back.

"Your goof," Grant responded as usual.

"My goof. Yes, mine." They fell asleep, holding each other, hearts in tune.

Chapter Eight

"Hey."

Grant forced his eyes open and saw that Jamie's face was right in front of him, those beautiful blue eyes shining brightly at him.

"Hey, yourself, gorgeous."

Jamie snorted at him, reached out to trace the contours of the side of Grant's face as it lay on the pillow. "Me? You're the one with such cool colours. Dark hair and light blue eyes. How did that happen? With those cheekbones and that silky hair, I'd almost think there was some American Indian in you, but the blue eyes are a surprise, a beautiful surprise. They're quite stunning, as my friend, Jonathon, would say. With him, everything is simply divine or quite stunning. Your eyes are both. The rest of you doesn't suck either." Jamie teased.

"Oh, really? I thought..." Grant started to joke, but Jamie caught him before he could finish.

"Well, only in the best possible way, of course." They both laughed and rolled together, arms going around each other.

"We need to get up," Grant said. "We've got to go get Brit this morning, and you've got to go to work. I've got therapy. Life comes back in big time today. But Jamie, I'll never, ever, forget yesterday and last night. You rocked my world with your actions and words."

"Hey, the same thing goes. I've never been this happy." Jamie nuzzled his face into Grant's neck, breathing in deeply. "Love the way you smell."

"Yeah, I know what you mean. That's what got me started last night, remember?"

Jamie growled, remembering, and nipped Grant's collarbone then kissed it better.

Grant got quiet for a moment. Jamie pulled back to look down at him.

"What's up? I can hear gears turning in there."

"I have to think about a job soon. Any ideas?"

"I've actually thought about it a little. You know Tony is director of one of the park systems here. Maybe you could get on there this summer then you'd have time to look for something else." Jamie leaned back, turning Grant onto his shoulder, his arm stretching over his back. "I'm not sure what he'd have, and you're not up to hard physical labour, but something light for the summer should be fine." He turned his head down to look into Grant's eyes. "You *are* thinking about staying here with me, aren't you?" He stopped, pushing them both up then put Grant back down on the bed and leaned over him "Wait, let me rephrase that. I'm asking you to move in here for good. Live with me, love with me, grow old with me. What do you think? Too soon?"

"Not for me. I told you I finally feel like I've found out who I am and what I want." He smiled up at Jamie, answering him seriously. "I'd love to live and love with you. I'll be a step-daddy to Brit, huh? I'll stand with you against Donnie and whatever he comes up with next. When's your next day off?" Grant asked, those gears working again.

"Not 'til Sunday, why? What are you planning?"

"I thought maybe we could invite Tony over for supper and talk to him about this summer. Get some ideas and some plans. If he doesn't have something, maybe he'll have some ideas." Grant leaned up on an elbow to be level with Jamie.

"It's time to take control of things and stop just letting things happen to me. I'm going to be a little more proactive. I also think we need to check back with the police and see why in the world they can't find Donnie and what has to happen before they consider it important enough to really work at looking."

"I like the way you think. You're right," Jamie said. "Let's ask Tony over for Sunday supper. Tell him we'll cook. We'll see if he thinks there's anything suitable available for you to do while you finish recuperating."

"Mmm 'kay," Grant said, reaching to smooth his hand over Jamie's head, cupping the back of his neck.

"I'll check in with Officer Johnson and see what we should do next. I don't feel right just sitting around waiting to see what Donnie will do. I want to know what they're doing to find him, and what it's going to take to stop him."

"Sounds like a plan. Now, how about a quick shower, a slow kiss then breakfast. After that, we'll go get Brit, get him settled in, and get started on other things."

* * * *

After bringing Brit home and watching him bound around happily checking out his territory again, Jamie and Grant got busy on the phone.

Jamie called the police station to see if he could talk to Officer Johnson. Luck was with him, and the officer was there and came on quickly.

"This is Jamie Taylor."

"Hey. Something else happen?" Officer Johnson was abrupt.

"No, sir. I'm calling for some information. I feel like we're sitting ducks here. We know Donnie's gonna do something else. Am I right that nothing can be done until he actually does something and gets caught doing it?"

"Basically that's right, Jamie. Until we can run him down on the charges we already have, it's just a wait and see. I've got a couple of different cars checking your place regularly, but until we catch him, I'm afraid you're vulnerable."

"Yes, sir. That's how we feel, vulnerable. Is there any way we can legally protect ourselves? To tell you the truth, I've even thought about getting a license for a gun. I won't have him hurting Grant or Brit."

"I can't advise you to do that, Jamie. I do think you need a better home security system. You've got a pretty good neighbourhood watch in your area. Maybe a couple of hidden cameras to catch anything that moves outside."

"Yeah, okay. I'll look into that. Any idea why you all can't find him? I mean is anybody really looking?" Jamie was frustrated that Donnie could get around and do his dirty work and never get caught.

"He hasn't been back to his apartment since this started. His father hasn't seen him nor have his neighbours. No one seems to know where he'd go to hide out."

"He's an odd one. I don't know of any friends he has or anything he does. He would just show up at work and always be around me. I never thought that much about it until it escalated recently...after Grant showed up and I became interested in him. Donnie evidently thinks he has a prior claim on me. That is not in any way true. We never even talked that much, especially about anything like that."

"I understand that. We *are* actively looking for him, but with no idea where to look, it's like the proverbial needle." The officer's voice showed he was frustrated, too.

They hung up soon.

Jamie looked over to Grant, who had finished his call to Tony and waited for him to finish with the officer. They shared their information.

Grant started, since his was quick and easy. "Tony said he'd be happy to join us for supper. He's bringing dessert. He said he'd check on what was available for the summer and we'd talk about it then."

Jamie relayed what he had learned from Officer Johnson. They talked about getting some cameras set up in front and back of the house and discussed everyone's frustration with being unable to find Donnie.

Jamie went to work and since Grant had already been to therapy today, he stayed to play with Brit. He was going through the kitchen to the back door when he saw a note on the table. Ah! He loved the fact that Jamie often left notes for him. He never knew where he'd find them—sometimes in the underwear drawer, the freezer, under a coaster in the living room, on the fridge, under his pillow. He got a kick out of it, especially because Jamie always ended the notes with the words *Love, Jamie*.

Grant got a little shiver every time he read those words. Loving and being loved was something totally new to him and he revelled in all the different ways they'd found to show each other how they felt. This note merely said that Jamie couldn't wait to see him later that night and was signed with the usual, heart-stopping words. Grant beamed as he went out the door with Brit.

They'd been playing for a while in the backyard when suddenly Brit went crazy. He ran right for the gate, growling and scratching at the wood. Grant hurried over and managed to push Brit out of the way and opened the gate. Brit shot past him, and Grant hurried down the drive, calling for Brit to come back. He got to the end just in time to see a dark car peeling away around the corner. Damn! Donnie again, no doubt. He called for Brit to come back. The dog stood at the edge of Jamie's yard, quivering and whimpering. He looked like he wanted a piece of Donnie and wasn't happy that he'd missed his chance.

"Come on, boy. Let's go back and lock up. He didn't get a chance to do anything today. Good boy, Brit. Come on, now." Brit came over and they walked back up the drive and into the backyard, closing and locking the gate. Damn! Jamie was gonna shit when he heard.

Grant went in and called the station to report what had happened then he called Jamie at work to tell him. He'd hated calling Jamie at work but knew better than to wait until he got home to tell him about Donnie's latest attempt. He told Jamie over and over things were fine. They had handled everything, and no one was hurt. He insisted Jamie stay at work, and he'd see him when he got home.

The next morning Jamie and Grant went to a local technology store and got a couple of easy cameras and instructions on setting them up. Before Jamie went to work that day the cameras were up and running. He'd borrowed a neighbour's tall ladder to put them high enough that Donnie couldn't just disarm them if he happened to see them.

* * * *

Donnie was able to sneak into the centre and make his way to the room he planned to visit tonight. Miss Wilhemina was Jamie's favourite. Everyone knew it. What he would do tonight would put a hurt on Jamie for sure. He almost smiled thinking of the how Jamie would react when he heard.

He almost allowed himself a chuckle as he slipped into Miss Wilhemina's room. There she was, her bed by the window. He slipped over and picked up a pillow and stood by her bed looking down at her. Old people creeped him out.

Unbeknownst to Donnie, Miss Wilhemina was like a lot of the elderly. She slept very little. She mostly rested at night. She saw him standing over her and was afraid her life was about to be over. She instinctively knew it wasn't a tech or someone there to do something nice for her. There was an aura of menace about him. Her hand slid over just a little, and she pressed the button for help.

She started to bring her hand up just as the pillow came down on her face. She had nowhere near the strength necessary to move it away.

* * * *

"Miss Wilhemina, hon, whatcha need? It's Todd. Saw your light on and...*Hey*! What the *hell*! *Help*! Get some help in here!" The tech who had come in from the hall after seeing Miss Wilhemina's light come on darted over to her bed to grab the pillow. He didn't take time to try to grab Donnie. He wanted to make sure she was okay. Out of the corner of his eye, he saw Donnie dart out, heard someone shout out in the hall, but he was already calling for more help for Miss Wilhemina.

People showed up in a hurry. Some chased Donnie. Some headed for the room. Todd checked her vitals and finding that she was gasping for breath and her heart was racing. Well, hell, why not? Several people worked over her, making sure she was going to be okay. This was attempted murder. No one doubted that.

All she was able to say was, "It was that Donnie. It was Donnie."

They spent a lot of time with her, taking great care with her, pampering her, loving on her a little. She was everyone's favourite. Finally, she said something that had them all pausing a moment.

"Oh, this is gonna upset Jamie so much. I hate that."

Todd slipped out and made the call. He didn't know what had happened, if anyone had been able to catch Donnie or if he'd gotten away. Bastard.

"Jamie? It's Todd. Uh, I've got something to tell you."

"Shit. What?"

"It's Miss Wilhemina. Donnie snuck in her room and, well, Jamie, he tried to smother her with a pillow. She saw him and was able to push the button. She's fine. She's worried about you being upset. She said that it was Donnie."

Todd had to pull the phone away from his ear as Jamie let fly with his very loud response to the news.

****

"Jamie, my God, what's the matter?" Grant asked when he heard Jamie's extreme language.

"Let's go. Get Brit. We're going to the centre."

"Okay. What...?" Grant started to ask, hopping up from the couch, totally mystified.

"I'm not leaving you here, and I've got to go check on Miss Wilhemina. Shit!""

"Jamie, tell me. Come on, man, you're scaring me." Grant grabbed Jamie's arm and stopped his frantic movements towards the door.

"Donnie tried to kill her. Grant, he tried to *kill her!* That sweet little old...wonderful little...he tried to smother her, Grant. How do I process that?"

"No way!"

"Yes fucking way! Todd saw her light on and went in and found Donnie over her bed. He got away. She's okay...they say...I've got to go. Come on with me, okay? Here, I'll get Brit's vest, and he'll go see her, too. That might even help calm her down. Todd said she was worried about me, bless her heart. I'm gonna kill him, Grant. I swear."

Jamie was so freaked out he shook. He couldn't believe what Todd told him. How could anyone, even Donnie, hurt that little old lady?

"Jamie, come here a sec." Grant opened his arms, and Jamie went right into them, shaking from head to toe with rage and fear and adrenaline. Grant squeezed as hard as he could. It was what he'd needed. Jamie knew Grant was trying to get him grounded enough to go do what they had to do.

"Thanks. I know I'm freaking. Let's move, though." He patted Grant on the shoulder and headed for Brit's vest. He snapped it on, knowing Brit would go into service mode when he saw Miss Wilhemina. He grabbed the keys and locked the house. In seconds, they were in the car and headed towards the centre.

In record time, they were walking down the hall towards Miss Wilhemina's room. There were several people standing around outside the door. He was relieved to see Officer Johnson there as well as others from the police station. They were talking to Todd and a couple of the other staff people. Todd caught sight of Jamie and pointed to the three of them coming rapidly down the hall.

Evidently Jamie's feelings were clear on his face because Officer Johnson stepped up to try and calm him down before he got to the door.

"Now son, you've got to..."

"What I've *got to do* is see Miss Wilhemina. Right now. Don't stop me. I'll talk to you in a minute, but I've got to see she's all right." Jamie felt like his last meal was coming up, and he was shaking right off his bones.

The matter was taken out of his hands when they heard a weak but determined voice from inside the room.

"Is that Jamie out there? Jamie, come on in here, sweet boy."

The officer stepped back and let Jamie, Grant, and Brit go in the room. There were a couple of nurses, a doctor and a policewoman in with her. They stepped out as the three walked into the room. Jamie just stood a moment, raking her from head to toe, making sure she really was all right.

"Well, don't just stand there, hon. Come over here and give me a hug. I'm fine. Now, you just stop worrying." She raised her arms up, and he was at her side immediately. She really was so dear to him.

He sat on the side of her bed and leaned down so she could reach him, and she brought him right down to her. His head rested beside hers, and she put one hand on the back of his head and rubbed it. He felt like sobbing, he was so distraught. Look what the mess in his life had done to her. It had nearly killed her.

"Stop it now. I know you feel responsible, but..."

He drew back, and there were tears in his eyes, but he sucked it up.

"It's my fault. He hates me, and he's hurting anyone and anything dear to me. He tried to kill Brit, and he started that fire in Grant's room and now this. I am totally responsible. It's all on me. I can never tell you how..."

"Now you listen here young man. Look at me, and hear me. You are not responsible for what someone else does. He is responsible. Only him. Don't let him win this...this...whatever it is. He's nothing compared to you. I've lived a long time, and I know people. *You* are someone of great worth."

He tried to duck his head, feeling bad at her words of praise for him when he felt so bad about what his situation had caused. She was having none of it.

"Jamie, give me your attention. Look at me, please." She put her hand on his cheek, drawing it back up so she could look in his eyes. "That's a good boy, no hanging your head. Don't let him make you doubt yourself. You are innately good. It is a joy and a privilege to know you. I want you to focus on making sure the important people in your life are safe now." She held her finger up to stop him from interrupting. "Don't worry about this. Don't let it bog you down. I know you. I know you feel responsible but just stop. For me, stop right now, and let me say hello to your young man." She reached for Grant's hand, and her eyes brightened when she saw Brit waiting patiently.

"Oh, I see you brought Brit to see me. Sit me up a little higher, will ya, honey? Can he get up here with me?"

She knew it wasn't in the rules, but she shamelessly used her situation to get her way. Like there was anyone on earth, much less in this centre, who would deny her anything she wanted right then.

Jamie turned, gave Brit the order to relax and patted the bed where he was. He got up and let Brit take his place. The big dog took the greatest care getting up onto the bed, and very carefully stretched out so that his head was right near Miss Wilhemina's. She could easily reach him to rub or lean a little to nuzzle his face. He whined a little and licked her cheek. She giggled like a little girl and looked up at Jamie, her face just beaming.

"Hello Grant. How are you, Handsome?"

Grant blushed, and Jamie teased them both.

"Miss Wilhemina, are you flirting? Young lady, it is after midnight and you need to think about resting, not getting all excited because there's a handsome man in the room."

As Grant leaned over to give her a kiss on the cheek, Jamie heard her say, "I'd say there's more than one handsome man in the room, wouldn't you?"

"Yes, ma'am. I would." Grant leaned in a little closer to her and whispered to her. "You know he loves you, don't you?"

Miss Wilhemina's eyes filled with tears, and she brought a hand up to her mouth. She looked right up into Grant's face and nodded her head.

Jamie teased them again. "Are you all keeping secrets now?"

"No, I don't really think it's a secret," Grant said, smiling with Miss Wilhemina. She patted the bed on her other side and Grant sat down.

"Now boys, you listen to me. I'm old as the hills, and my body is failing me over and over, but my mind is fine. I know exactly why that idiot was in here trying to snuff me out." She paused at when she saw the smiles on their faces, despite the topic. "What? Oh, the term? Okay, it dates me, but it means the same thing. I know he's crazy, and he's jealous of your special caring for each other. That's his problem. You don't let his meanness stop you from living your lives."

"But, he could have..." Jamie couldn't just ignore what had happened to her.

"Killed me? Yeah, I know. I imagine they'll step up the security around here now, and I'll be fine. I'm due to leave pretty soon. I'm doing so much better. You need to see what you can do to help them catch him before he really does kill somebody. Go on now. I need to get some sleep tonight. You come see me tomorrow, and I'll be fine. Just be extra careful 'til they catch him, okay?"

"I know it's stupid, but I'm afraid to leave you alone." Jamie knew it sounded silly. Lord knew she wouldn't be alone, but she was so old, tiny, frail and sweet.

"You could leave Brit with me...just for tonight." Oh, the pleading in her voice. She was really playing him.

"Brit, stay. Guard." Jamie didn't even think about it. He'd feel better with Brit there with her. He went out into the hall and motioned for Todd to come over. He explained, and Todd agreed to take Brit out a couple times during the rest of the night and get someone to take over early in the morning until Jamie got there for work.

Jamie leaned over and kissed Miss Wilhemina good night then patted Brit on the head before motioning for Grant to join him in the hall. He knew he had more talking to do with the police and staff waiting for him. He could do it now that he'd seen she was all right.

Officer Johnson was waiting. The others had gone about their business. Jamie suggested they go to the cafeteria, get some coffee and sit down to figure out what to do.

"I can't just sit around and wait to see who he's going after next. Hell, you've got him for three attempted murders now. You know he could have killed Grant and others when he set that fire in there and he tried to kill Brit and now Miss Wilhemina. Everybody here knows how I feel about her. I love that little old lady. You've got to find him. Catch him, put him away."

Setting his coffee on the table in front of him, Officer Johnson nodded.

"I swear to you, Jamie, we're looking. He's got to have someone hiding him. He's not at any of the places we've been told he's likely be. We've got people watching his apartment and his father's house. His father had agreed to turn him in if he shows up. This has taken a toll on *that* man, let me tell you." The officer shook his head, obviously thinking about Mr. Wilkins and the heartache of turning in one's son for the crimes that Donnie had stacked up.

"It's not something we've put on the back burner. We are actively looking," he assured the two men.

"Maybe I should..." Jamie paused as his cell phone rang in his pocket. He reached for it. Grant watched his face to see if he could tell who was calling this late. Jamie jumped up, knocking back his chair back and yelled. "I'm coming."

Both men stood and Grant asked, "What's he done now?"

"The fire department is at the house. It seems there's a bonfire in my backyard."

"What? That doesn't make sense."

"Sure it does," Officer Johnson said. "He's showing you he can get in anywhere, anytime, and wreak havoc. He's gonna make a mistake and get caught soon. Come on, I'll go with you."

They saw the crowd as they turned onto their street. The fire truck was there as well as many of the neighbours. Jamie and Grant hurried to the back of the house. The smell was still strong.

Everything from the backyard was piled into the middle and burned. All the picnic tables, chairs, benches and so on from the party the other night were now black and smouldering. There was a large burned area of grass around the mess in the middle of the yard.

Suddenly, Grant said, "Cameras. Jamie, it should all be on camera. One of them is pointed so it gets the whole back yard."

Officer Johnson had one of his men gather all the equipment so they could take it in and go over it. Of course, it wouldn't tell them where he was hiding, but it sure would be evidence in the growing list of felonies against the man.

It was late when Jamie and Grant finally headed for bed, or early, as the case may be. They'd hit the shower for a quick wash then fallen into bed, arms wrapped around each other. Sleep claimed them, despite the many things warring for lead spot in their thoughts.

Jamie awoke midmorning. He turned to look down at Grant who still slept heavily. His heart turned over as he gazed at his lover. Beautiful, sexy, strong, sexy...okay. Letting him rest, Jamie got up, dressed quietly and left the room after one more glance at Grant's body, stretched out and looking so...sexy.

He opened the backdoor, and the smell hit him. Just like a snap of the fingers, his good dreamy feelings upon waking were wiped out. He looked at the charred remains of his backyard furniture and frowned. What was he going to do? Just wait for Donnie to do something worse. Hell, what could be worse than trying to kill everyone he loved?

He sat down on the steps of the patio, the only place left to sit and tried to think of ways he could trap Donnie. It was obvious that Donnie was trying to get to him. He hated to think he was being like all those TV shows, but he was about to try to set himself up as bait. Stupid, maybe. But he couldn't let this continue.

"There I was sleeping like a baby, and this awful noise from back here woke me up." Grant's voice was low and rumbly, right behind him.

"Hey, Handsome." Jamie teased him with Miss Wilhemina's name for him.

"Funny. How are you this morning?" Grant moved his hand over Jamie's head. He sat down beside Jamie. "I kept hearing this grinding noise from out here and realised it was the gears inside here that were going full blast."

"Ha. Ha. I thought I'd let you sleep a little. I've been sitting here trying to figure out how to draw Donnie out."

"Whoa! If you're thinking of being bait for him, you can just…"

"What, Grant? Just what? Wait for him to kill you, Brit, Tony, another neighbour? Come on, you know this has to stop, and it's me he's fixated on. It makes perfect sense."

"So I just let him kill you instead?"

"Well, that wasn't what I was thinking. I was going more for setting him up." Jamie leaned over and bumped shoulders with Grant. "I'm not stupid. I intend to run it by Officer Johnson, but I'm going to meet Donnie head on from now on, not sit back and wait for him to hurt someone else. Let's draw him to us and take him down. You know, before he can snuff out anyone else?"

Grant laughed with him as he'd wanted. Jamie turned and took Grant's lips while they were open and happy. Grant turned into him and the kiss deepened. Jamie put his feet down on a lower step and reached to pull Grant over onto his lap.

"Mmm, yeah, mmm…wait," Grant said and stood a second to turn and sit down facing Jamie, straddling his legs. It was a little awkward with Grant's long legs sticking straight out behind Jamie. His knee was still tight so he had to make accommodations for it, but finally they had a good fit. Grant put his arms around Jamie's neck and leaned in to finish what they'd started.

Jamie slid his tongue right back into Grant's ready mouth. It was what he needed to ground him and get his mind back to what was important—them. He swirled his tongue around Grant's mouth, tangling and teasing with Grant's. When he sucked hard on Grant's tongue, he got a low rumble in response. He repeated the action a few times and soon had a squirming man on his legs, humping up into his cock. Yeah, like that.

Jamie reached down and rubbed against Grant's hard cock, earning another deep rumble.

He eased back a little to say, "You're awfully rumbly this morning. It's very sexy." Jamie leaned back in for more tongue. This time, he pushed his into Grant's mouth, and Grant returned the favour, sucking hard and getting a happy jerk from Jamie.

Jamie's hands went right to Grant's hips and pulled him in tighter. He began rubbing them together, creating a wonderful friction, cock against cock. Mmm, that's what he was talking about.

"More…oh, Jamie. That's good. Feels good…" Grant managed to say.

"'S'posed to. Move back just a little. I wanna touch you," Jamie said, against Grant's lips.

"Out here?" Grant's shock tickled Jamie and he laughed out loud.

"Why not? The cameras are gone, the fence is high, we're all alone…come on, you know you want to…"

Jamie hadn't finished talking before Grant was easing back, standing carefully, dropping his shorts then crossing his arms, waiting.

When Jamie looked up in surprise and bewilderment, Grant laughed back at him and said, "Am I going to be the only one naked out here?"

Jamie snorted in laughter. He put his hands on Grant's hips to hold on and stood up, which put them right against each other. Grant placed his hands on Jamie's waist, slid his fingers under the band of Jamie's shorts and pushed them down. When Jamie stepped out of them, Grant reached around and placed the shorts on the step for Jamie to sit on. His, he put down beside Jamie to rest his sore knee on and then pushed against Jamie's shoulder, indicating he should sit back down.

"What about your knee, babe? I don't want to hurt you…"

"Shh, I know what I can handle. Besides, I don't think this will take long, not with the way I'm feeling."

They settled and after a few seconds of rearranging, their cocks were rubbing together, held fast in Grant's hand. Jamie had his arms around Grant to make sure he was steady on his lap. The tight friction of Grant's hand and his cock against Jamie's had him groaning and pushing up towards Grant.

"For someone who's relatively new to this," Jamie panted, "you have an amazing ability for variety. Imagination?"

"Inspiration." That got Grant an open-mouthed kiss that took them both into joint climax. Grant's hand held them together and when they both came, he kept moving, smearing their combined cum over their now ultra-sensitive cocks.

"Mmmm, taste?" Jamie requested. Grant stopped his movements and looked into Jamie's eyes. He brought his hand up and put it between their mouths. They both worked together to clean it up, never taking their eyes from each other's. Once the hand was bathed, Grant put it on the back of Jamie's neck and pulled. They shared the flavours in another tongue-thrusting kiss that had both moaning and squirming.

"God, you're sexy," Jamie said. "That's what I was thinking when I watched you sleep this morning before coming out here. You are so sexy."

"You, too. I love you, Jamie," Grant said, before laying his head on Jamie's shoulder and sighing heavily. Happiness and peace, for a few minutes at least.

Jamie wondered why they couldn't just stay like this? Why did they have to deal with some psycho trying to bust up the best thing he'd ever had? But they did.

"You want to go with me to talk to Officer Johnson this morning? I'm not stupid. I'm not going all Rambo and trying to take this guy down by myself. You can relax. But I'm not sitting here waiting for him to strike again without some kind of plan, either."

"I'm with you, Jamie. Anything you say. You're right, we can't just let him keep hurting people like this. Let's shower, call and see if he's there, grab some food and go see him, then Miss Wilhemina. How's that for a plan?"

"Sounds pretty complete," Jamie said, holding on as Grant stood, a little stiff from the odd position. He took a little time to make sure that his lover was steady before bending to grab their shorts and taking Grant's hand as they went back in.

"By the way, I had a thought," Grant said, waiting a second to get Jamie's attention.

"What's that, hon?"

"I heard Miss Wilhemina say she was about to be released from the centre. Do you think we could have her over for supper sometime? I think she'd like that. She's probably lonely where she lives and…well, she loves you and Brit and…" Grant trailed off, hoping he didn't sound silly.

Jamie grabbed him and pushed their mouths together in a kiss of love, gratitude and pure happiness. "You…you continue to amaze me. I love you for the way you think, the way you fit me so well, fit into my life, fit into me pretty well, too. Come here." He drew Grant to the bathroom and bent to start the shower. He dropped both pairs of shorts into the hamper and pulled Grant in with him. He settled Grant against the wall, dropped down to his knees and took Grant into his mouth, loving the shocked gasp then the heady moan that followed. He proceeded to let Grant know what he thought of the way he fit both him and his life.

Chapter Nine

Jamie was pleased that the next week was relatively quiet. Grant and Brit were home with him. Miss Wilhemina had, indeed, left the rehab centre for the assisted living home where she lived. They met with Tony, and he was looking into finding something for Grant that summer. Jamie would have been completely happy, except for a niggling feeling that the other shoe was about to fall.

Jamie and Grant had met with Officer Johnson and discussed possible ways for finding and apprehending Donnie before he could do more harm. Both Jamie and Grant were carrying disks in their pockets that would summon the police at the touch of a button. The disks were similar to the lifeline things older people who lived alone wore. These, though, would be activated only if immediate help was needed from the police force.

Friday night found them both home as it was Jamie's day off. They had cleared the mess from the backyard and replaced the basics of the yard furniture. The patio furniture they'd chosen for comfort as well as function. The loungers were large enough for two. The table and chairs were large and big enough for friends to sit around and enjoy each other's company. They'd cooked steaks on the grill, along with large-cut veggies. They were topping it off with warm brownies, covered with a fudge-like icing.

"I can't believe how rich this is," Jamie said, taking a big bite and turned it so Grant could take one also. "It's been a while since I was this happy. I'm glad you're here to share this with me."

"Me, too, so glad." Grant leaned in to place his chocolaty lips against Jamie's.

They both jerked when Brit scrambled up from beside them and flew off the patio, barking and running for the gate of the fence. They both jumped up, looking at each other.

"Brit! Come back here, boy!" Jamie yelled, running towards the gate. He wasn't taking a chance that it was Donnie, going for Brit again.

Brit wasn't minding him but instead scratched at the gate, growling and barking fiercely, trying to get out. Jamie grabbed his collar and dragged him back towards the patio and Grant. Brit pulled against him the whole way, obviously wanting to get free and go back to the gate.

"I'm putting him inside, then, I'll check it out," Jamie explained to Grant. Grant waited 'til Jamie was inside the house before he headed for the gate to see what had Brit so excited. He couldn't see anything through the slats in the privacy fence. He hesitated about opening the gate since he wasn't prepared to handle Donnie if he was there with a weapon.

Jamie came flying off the patio towards him.

"What are you doing? Get back from there!"

"Jamie, chill. I'm not Brit. I was waiting for you. Now, come on. Let's see what's so interesting out there." Jamie grabbed him and gave him a quick hug.

"I'm sorry. I just got scared thinking of something else happening to you."

"It's okay. We're in this together now. Come on." Grant reached to unlock the gate. He stepped back, and Jamie took hold of the side of it and flung it back, expecting to see Donnie on the other side. Instead, there was a note tacked to the front of the gate with a pocketknife. It read: *Come on inside, boys. I'm waiting for you.*

Jamie took a second to glance at Grant, horror dawning on his face. Inside! His house? With Brit? Shit! How...?

They both took off running for the back door. Grant grabbed his arm before they got within sight of the backdoor. He reached into his pocket and grabbed the button and gestured for Jamie to take his out, too. Jamie nodded, and they both pushed the buttons at the same time, silently requesting that the police come. They both put them back in their pockets before they headed into the house, easing the backdoor open and softly closing it.

Jamie didn't hear anything, though he should have heard Brit. He motioned for Grant to ease over with him to a drawer with knives in it. He hadn't gone out and bought a gun, but he wasn't facing Donnie without some kind of weapon. Grant put a small, very sharp, paring knife the back pocket of his shorts, giving Jamie one, too. Jamie put it his pocket, like

Grant, then took a large chef's knife out, mostly for show. Donnie would see it but not expect them to have small ones hidden.

Jamie reached out and touched Grant's shoulder, quickly, and said, "I love you. Let's don't do anything stupid."

"Right back at ya," Grant replied, and they turned towards the hall leading to the rest of the house.

"Brit, come here, boy. Where are you?" Jamie stood still and listened. He heard a short whimper, quickly muffled, coming from the bedroom. He looked over at Grant and knew they were thinking the same thing. Bastard! He hated that Donnie was in their room.

They both walked to the doorway of the room and looked in. Donnie sat on the side of the bed with his arms wrapped around Brit's neck, holding it up in an awkward position, making it hard for him to breathe. Brit was held tight and seemed to know not to struggle.

Jamie's instinct was to rush over and free Brit, but the evil smile and the shiny silver gun pressed against Brit's head held Jamie firmly in place. He was so furious he wanted to growl.

"What do you want, Donnie? How in the *hell* did you get in here?" Jamie exploded, shaking with rage.

"Aw, not glad to see me? I gather you've been looking for me, huh, Jamie boy? Oh, hi Grant. How's it hangin'?" Donnie looked from Jamie to Grant and took his gun hand away from Brit's head for a second. He put it back as Jamie started forward, though.

"Uh-uh. You don't want to piss me off, Jamie. I couldn't care less if Whistlebutt here dies or not. You know, it's a shame that poor old Miss Willy isn't here.

I could take care of all of them at the same time. I'd get most everyone you love at one time. God, that'd make me feel good. Drop the cleaver. Now!" His eyes gleamed as he talked about hurting everyone in Jamie's life.

"Why are you doing this? Just tell me." Jamie sounded resigned, though he was perfectly alert. He dropped the chef's knife as he'd expected to do.

"You know. You've felt it, too. You know the way I feel about you. I know you felt the same way about me before tall and gawky showed up. How could you go for him? Really? He's not as smart as I am."

"Right." Jamie couldn't help the sarcasm in his voice.

"What? You don't have the police looking for me? Have they been able to find me? No. Has anyone been able to stop me? No. I can do anything I want. Right now, I think I want your boy there to strip while I watch."

"What? You sick bastard, no way," Jamie yelled, starting for Donnie. He didn't know what he was going to do, but he was through with this.

"Ah-ah! Back up, unless you want me to shoot this mutt's brains all over your wall. That's right, back up. Now, how much do you love your precious dog, huh? Enough to let me have a go at pretty boy, there?" Donnie motioned with his gun at Grant, standing wide-eyed beside Jamie.

Jamie's heart was surely going to pound right out of his chest. Hell, where were the police? He didn't know how long it would take for them to get here.

"It's all right, Jamie. We won't let anything happen to Brit." Grant stepped up a little in front of Jamie.

"So, Donnie, you looking for a straight strip or you want a show?"

Jamie was the one wide-eyed now. He couldn't believe Grant had said that. What was he *do*ing? Jamie looked at Grant and knew Grant could see the dismay on his face. Grant put his hand to his pocket and rubbed. Shit. Of course, the disks! Grant was telling him that he was stalling for time so the police could get here. Smart…foolish man. God, if Donnie did anything to hurt Grant, Donnie was gonna die right here…tonight. Jamie played along with Grant.

"Come on, Grant, you don't have to do this." He put a little pleading into his voice. He tried to hide his fury from Donnie. The way he felt, he could kill the bastard with his bare hands right now.

"No biggie, Jamie. Hey, Donnie, will you let Brit go if I do what you want? You…" Jamie could tell he was making his voice quiver "You're not gonna really hurt me, are you?" Jamie knew Grant was making his fury sound like fear.

"Well, we'll see. Here, Jamie, take your damn dog!" Donnie threw Brit away from him. Brit immediately turned on him, growling and baring his teeth, ready to tear into him.

"Brit!" Jamie yelled. "Over here, boy. Now." Brit stopped instantly and turned to look at Jamie as if to say, "Are you crazy? This is the guy who hurt me!"

"Now, Brit," Jamie said, slapping his leg as Donnie raised his gun hand to hit Brit. Brit jumped away and came to Jamie. "Sit," Jamie ordered and Brit obeyed, though he quivered from head to tail with his need to protect them.

"Everybody happy now?" Donnie sneered. "Let's see what ya got that makes Jamie slobber like he does over you. Come on—what? Do you need music?" Donnie gestured to Grant, indicating he should get on with the strip show he waited for. Jamie could tell he liked his role as puppet master.

Grant reached for the top button of his shirt, and Jamie had a moment to be glad he'd worn a button down shirt today. He approved of the slow way Grant went from button to button, taking off the shirt. Hell, when it was the two of them, Grant just pulled it over his head.

"Really, Jamie, what do you see in him? He's awfully skinny. I've thought about taking him out, you know. Then you'd turn to me. You would, you know. I'm the only one who knows you. We've got something special between us." Donnie rambled on, his eyes going back and forth between Grant and Jamie. "No, don't stop. Now, the pants. Lose 'em." Donnie gestured with the gun, making Jamie's heart stop as it wavered in front of him, pointing at Grant.

Grant looked at Jamie now, his heart in his eyes. Jamie saw fear and resolve and resignation in them. Jamie could tell Grant was determined to follow his plan to give them time for the police to get there, but he was surely worried about how far this would go.

"How'd you get in here, Donnie?" Jamie hoped to distract him from Grant.

Donnie switched his attention to Jamie, eager to show off his superior skills.

"I wondered when you'd ask. Your front door's too easy. You think you're so smart. The lock's broken and the alarm isn't working right anymore. I've got tricks of my own, ya know." Donnie put his gun hand down on the bed and looked at Jamie now, getting into his conversation. "You never gave me enough credit. I always felt like you were blowing me off, like you didn't think I was smart enough for you. I showed you, didn't I?"

Jamie was amazed that Donnie was crazy enough to think he would applaud his smart thinking as he held a gun on Grant and made him strip. After all the things Donnie had done to hurt others in Jamie's life, Jamie figured the man really was out of his mind.

Suddenly, Donnie caught on that Grant had stopped and he'd been lax with the gun, setting his hand down on the bed. He brought up the gun and pointed it towards Grant. With an evil smirk, he moved his hand a little to the right and pulled the trigger. They all jumped at the loud sound. Brit sprang at Donnie. Jamie jumped for Grant, taking him to the floor. He heard Donnie yelling for Brit to get off him. There was another shot and a yelp from Brit. Jamie and Grant both scrambled to get up from the tangle they were in on the floor.

"Brit!" Jamie yelled, finally getting up and heading for the pair by the bed.

He took in the scene quickly. Brit had his mouth firmly around Donnie's arm, and Donnie was yelling, jerking the arm, trying to dislodge the strong hold Brit had on him. He repeatedly hit Brit with the gun, but Brit wasn't letting go. Jamie had completely forgotten the knife he'd been forced to drop earlier. He scooped it up and lunged for Donnie.

Grant surged off the floor and threw himself onto Donnie's arm, the one with the gun. He put his shoulder against Donnie's, pushing him back onto the bed. He used both arms to hold the gun in Donnie's hand against the bed.

The shock of having the dog and both men attack him made Donnie an easy target. Grant finally got the gun away, Brit still had hold of Donnie's bleeding arm, refusing to release it, and Jamie stood over him with the big knife in his raised hand. Donnie screamed like a girl just as the police burst into the room.

"I'll kill you all," Donnie screamed, then his voice slid right into a whine. "Get off me, get him off. Owwwww!" His voice was high and loud now.

There was a noise at the door.

"Freeze. Drop it, sir."

Jamie turned to find men pouring into the room, guns drawn, all pointing at him. Perfect.

"Glad you could make it," Jamie said, lowering his hand slowly, dropping the knife again. He put his hands on his hips. He refused to raise them. Jamie turned to see Grant was standing still, his hands down to his sides, looking from Donnie to the officers with the guns still aimed at him.

From the bed, Donnie still squealed like a whiny girl. "Get him off me. He's gonna kill me. Help me, dammit."

Jamie turned to the bed. "Brit, release. Come here, boy." Brit immediately opened his jaws and let Donnie go and stepped over to Jamie and sat. He was limping and there was blood on his leg. Jamie bent quickly and saw that he'd been shot in the leg. It was a graze, just a shear across his skin, but damnit! He stood and walked over to the bed where Donnie was cradling his arm and whining.

"Hey!" Jamie yelled and Donnie looked up. Jamie drew his arm back, prepared to throw a roundhouse punch in the hopes of taking Donnie's head off. Bastard! He felt arms grab him and pull him back and heard Grant yelling for them to let him go, but he didn't care. Damnit! That would have felt so good.

"Where's Officer Johnson? Is he here?" Jamie asked, looking around the group.

"He's off tonight, but…"

"Call him…please." Jamie knew the officer would want to know about this.

One of the officers nodded to another who pulled out a phone and started punching in a number. Another couple stood over Donnie. The ones who'd grabbed Jamie away from Donnie had finally let him go and stood looking around.

"Start talking," said one of the officers.

"Can I put my shirt back on?" Grant asked. That got Jamie's attention immediately. He turned and grabbed Grant and pulled him into his arms.

"Are you all right?" He tried to move his hands over Grant to make sure he was all in one piece. He'd been so scared that Donnie would kill Grant. He'd shot at him! "Are you? Grant, tell me, you're okay."

"Jamie, I'm fine. He missed me." Grant squeezed Jamie hard then pushed him away a little. "I don't think he meant to hit me. I saw him move the gun over, away from me. I think he was just trying to scare us."

"Worked. Scared the *shit* outta me." Jamie was still furious.

"Is someone going to tell me what's going on here?" the officer said, obviously deciding he'd waited patiently enough.

"Yes, sir. We arranged with the court to have a restraining order against him, but no one was ever able to catch up with him to serve it on him. There are several reports at the station relating to this man, Donnie Wilkins. He's been stalking Jamie," Grant spoke up, pointing to Donnie and Jamie respectively.

"Yeah? This is that guy? We've heard about him for a few weeks now. Been looking all over for him." The officer showed more interest now. Jamie wished Officer Johnson or the other one, Mark Thomas, was here. He started explaining.

"He slashed my tires, he started a fire in Grant's room at the rehab centre when he was still there, he painted filth on my front door, he poisoned my dog, he tried to smother a sweet old lady with a pillow, just because I love her, he started a fire in my backyard...is that enough? We've known all along he was doing it. I did my part to get a restraining order against him, but you all couldn't *find* him. He didn't have any trouble finding us over and over!" The more Jamie talked, the madder he got.

"Interesting list. Is there a reason for his actions?"

"Ask him. I can't figure it out. He's swears there's something between us, but I'm here to tell you there never has been. He's delusional. I can't stand him. I never could. When Grant came to the centre Donnie went crazy, threatening us every time we turned around, even before Grant and I got together." Jamie reached for Grant's hand. Now that the panic was over, he just needed to touch him. Well, he needed *more*, but that could wait.

"So this is a lover's quarrel then?" one of the officers asked, sneering.

Grant grabbed Jamie's arm and held tight. It was clear to everyone that Jamie was not in the mood to be talked to like that right now. A noise at the door surprised them all. Jamie turned to find Officer Johnson stepping in, obviously just in time to hear the last comment.

"Officer Bunch, you and Jenkins take Mr. Wilkins to the station. I guess you better stop at the hospital and have that arm looked at. If you let him get away from you, I'll have both your badges. Count on it. Now go!"

They all watched as the two officers marched Donnie out the door to put him in the cruiser. Officer Johnson turned back to Jamie and Grant.

"I'm glad you had me called. Are you both okay? What's wrong with Brit? Is he bleeding?"

"Donnie shot him. It just grazed his leg, but I'll take him to see Doc Kevin in a little bit, soon as we're done here."

The officer bent to rub Brit's head and check out the place on the dog's leg. He nodded as he stood again.

"If you're sure he's okay. I'll wait if he needs help now," Officer Johnson said, kindly.

"No, he's fine. Go ahead. Ask your questions," Jamie said, gesturing into the living room. "Can we sit down, though? I'm suddenly feeling a little unsteady. Come on, Grant, you need to sit down, too."

Jamie led the way into the living room, and the three of them sat. There were sighs all around.

"Why don't you just tell me what happened?" Officer Johnson said, taking out a pad to write down notes.

They did, beginning with the meal on the patio and Brit flying off towards the gate, growling. They told about the note and finding Donnie and Brit in the bedroom, Donnie's demand for Grant to strip for him, the gunshot, and the fight that followed. The telling took a while.

"You've all had quite a night. Go on and take Brit in to the vet. I'll go in and process Donnie, making sure all of the previous reports aren't forgotten. He'll not see freedom for a long, long time. I'll contact his father." He shook his head, obviously thinking that making that call wouldn't be fun. "It'll be interesting to find out where he's been hiding all this time, too. Come down tomorrow, late morning, and I'll have information for you and forms for you to work on. I'm sorry it took so long to get him."

* * * *

Jamie called the vet and Kevin said he'd meet them at the office. They got Brit taken care of then headed back home, totally worn out. When they pulled up, they saw Tony waiting for them.

"Are you all okay? I've been assigned by the neighbourhood to check and get back to them." He reached down to pet Brit as he trotted up the steps to where Tony waited.

"We're fine. Come on in a minute. We'll explain. Then we're going to crash."

They told their story again and got hugs and congratulations from Tony. When they closed the door, with the broken lock, they just looked at each other for a moment.

"Let's go make that *our* room again. I want a long shower with lots of kisses then I need to hold you tight all night long. God, Grant, I can't believe it's over, all the fear and worry over what he'd do next." Jamie pulled Grant with him towards their room and the bathroom. He paused to touch the hole in the wall from Donnie's wayward bullet. He shivered as he remembered thinking Grant had been shot.

He reached out and took Grant into his arms, holding on tight. Grant must have realised what he was thinking, because he just held on and rocked Jamie back and forth.

"It's okay. I'm okay. He missed. I know what you must have thought, but I'm here, right where I'm supposed to be, in your arms. Let's go clean up and kiss each other a lot."

That's what Jamie needed, Grant, water and lots of kisses. Grant led him into the shower. They stripped and as their shorts hit the floor they heard clunking sounds and both realised at the same time what it was.

The little paring knives in their back pockets. Oops.

"It's a miracle we weren't sliced to ribbons with all that had happened tonight."

"Better let me check out that fine ass and make sure it's not hurt," Jamie said, turning Grant to look at his behind. He smoothed his hand over the firm globes, finding them still perfect…and sexy as hell.

"Seems to be none the worse for wear, how about mine?" Jamie asked, turning to present Grant with his own for inspection. He shivered as Grant moved his hands over his ass, ostensibly looking for any cuts made by the knife being in his back pocket all night. Evidently his was fine as well, if the satisfied hum from Grant was anything to go by.

He laughed, looking over his shoulder at Grant, then Grant was laughing with him and they stood, naked and giggling, in the bathroom. Jamie was just glad their pent up emotions were finding their release in laughter not tears. Things could have gone the other way.

"Come on, goofy. Let's get wet." He pulled Grant into the shower with him and turned on the jets. *Oh, now that felt good.* Not just the water. Grant was already smoothing the soapy loofah over his back and shoulders. He put his hands on the wall and dropped his head and let Grant take care of him. He'd return the favour in a few minutes. When Grant was finished, and a thorough job it was, Jamie turned and took him into his arms, rubbing their two very hard cocks together. That felt good, too.

Jamie took Grant's mouth in their first real kiss since the night's ordeal had begun. The kiss started out soft and slow but heated up rapidly. His tongue swept through Grant's mouth, gathering flavour and love. He thrust in and out in the rhythm that his hips had taken up below. Jamie decided they both needed sweet release. Taking one hand from Grant's neck, he reached down to take hold of both their cocks and hold them tightly together as he continued to thrust back and forth. The movement caused glorious friction between hands, cocks, and stomachs. They continued moving against each other, chests heaving as breathing grew harder. Jamie pulled away from Grant's mouth to look into his face. He found Grant looking back at him, just as seriously.

"I love you. Come on, baby. Come for me," he coaxed, leaning in to trace Grant's lips with his tongue. He wanted to go for sweet and corny but just couldn't sustain it. He delved back in and ground his lips against Grant's.

Jamie groaned into Grant's mouth, pushing his tongue inside and meeting Grant's for a feisty duel. Neither wanted sweet right now. They held on tight as both lost control at the same time, pulling away to put their heads into each other's necks and yelling with their releases.

"God, hold on to me. I'm not sure I can stand on my own," Jamie admitted, after he finally stopped shooting against Grant's stomach. He figured Grant felt the same way, if his breathing and the tight hold he had on Jamie was any indication. They stood in the hot spray and swayed just a little.

Finally, Jamie pulled away and turned so the shower would wash them clean. He took up the loofah and gave Grant a nice massaging wash. They stepped out of the shower, both feeling loose and tired.

* * * *

By mutual consent, they stripped the bed and remade it. Donnie had merely sat on top of the covers, but it just felt right to Jamie to change the bed, like they were erasing Donnie's presence. Actually, it was a wonder that there wasn't blood on the cover from

Donnie's arm, but it was clean. Regardless, they didn't put it back on. Just the sheet would be enough tonight.

"Come on, baby, I need you tonight." Jamie reached for Grant and pulled him down to the bed. They snuggled in and began slow kisses that developed into...more slow kisses.

"You feel so good. I love kissing you," Grant said. "What do you need tonight? You want to just go to sleep holding each other? Or would you like to fuck like bunnies as long as we can stay awake?"

"I like the sound of that last one," Jamie said, against Grant's neck. "I love loving you, but I swear, I'm so tired and just wasted. I don't know if it was the fear of losing you or all the excitement, but I want to just hold on to you. I want to cuddle, snuggle, whatever you want to call it. I just need to be close to you. I want to be still...and *close* to you." He finished and pulled his head from Grant's neck, wanting to see how Grant would take what he'd said.

"Mmm," Grant murmured, looking up into Jamie's eyes. "Perfect. I was afraid to tell you that's what I hoped for tonight. It just feels right."

Jamie drew Grant to him, and they snuggled together. He smiled as he felt Grant smoothing the top of his head, down his neck, and over his shoulders. He did a little of his own caressing, over the same areas on Grant's body. He heard the sigh Grant let go and smiled to himself again. They slept.

* * * *

"I think I'd like to go for that second choice now," Jamie said, into Grant's ear, sometime close to dawn.

"Mmm?" Grant turned his head to face Jamie. The small amount of light coming from the window was enough for Jamie to see Grant's smile.

"I don't think you're quite as out of it as you sound. What's the smile for?" Jamie teased.

"You. The smile's for you. I woke up to your voice in my ear and that's enough to make me smile, not to mention what you said." Grant scooted over and took Jamie into his arms and rubbed their stomachs together, twining their legs. "You needin', baby?"

"Need you. Last night, I needed to hold you. Now I need much, much more."

"I'm all yours." Grant threw himself back onto the bed, arms and legs spread, as if offering himself up for sacrifice. He turned his head to look at Jamie.

Jamie snorted at Grant's antics. "Silly man. No, stay there. I like that pose. Look at all that! Just for me?" He pounced, landing astraddle of Grant, his weight on his hands and knees. Grant laughed at him, reaching up and taking Jamie's face in his hands, bringing it down to his. Jamie went willingly, but he resisted the pull on his head just as he reached Grant's mouth. He was within millimetres of those perfect lips, breathing in, taking in Grant's breath, becoming one with him. Jamie put his tongue out gently, just touching Grant's top lip, sliding along to the corner of Grant's mouth. Grant's tongue came out to play, just grazing the tip of Jamie's. Jamie eased down, taking his weight onto his elbows and resting gently on Grant, not wanting to put his whole weight on him.

"It's okay, come on down here, lover. I want to feel you all over me," Grant whispered into Jamie's mouth.

"Sure?" Jamie murmured right back. When Grant nodded his head, it caused their lips to graze against each other again. Nice. Jamie took Grant at his word, and lowered himself to fit perfectly over Grant's body. Simultaneously, they squirmed a little, moving against each other. Jamie leaned a little further and took Grant's mouth fully.

He took great delight in Grant's moan of hunger. Jamie moved his tongue in and out of Grant's open lips, raking against his teeth, sliding over Grant's tongue, under it, around it, back and forth. He nearly growled with his sudden uncontrollable need to have Grant.

"What is it, Jamie? I can tell there's something..." Grant tried to ask, but Jamie just covered his mouth again, not wanting to put words to the feeling he had. He had his lover in his arms, but he could've lost him last night. He had to stake his claim, make Grant his again.

"I want you," Jamie managed to get out, taking Grant's mouth again, roughly, before Grant could say anything.

"Got me. I told you that. Hey, hold up a second. No, here, look at me, just a second." Grant eased back from Jamie a bit to look into his eyes. Jamie was afraid he could see the turmoil and a sort of wildness there.

"Tell me. What's got you so upset? I can tell the difference, you know," Grant said.

Jamie dropped his head to Grant's for a moment then put his arms around Grant's shoulders and rolled with him, pulling Grant on top of him.

"I almost lost you last night, and it's not that I didn't realise it then, or later, when we went to bed, I just..."

Jamie stopped, afraid he couldn't explain it right. "It suddenly hit me when we were kissing that it could have ended so differently. He could have killed you. What would I do? Grant, what would I do?"

Grant put his hands on the bed beside Jamie's head and pulled up to look down at Jamie. "Well, isn't it a good thing we're such a good team? We don't have to find out what you'd do without me. It's not gonna happen, baby. You're stuck with me, seriously stuck. Like, I'm not *ever* leavin' you. You better be sure you really want me around." Grant was obviously trying to turn the tables and make Jamie admit that they were both fine and would be now that the crisis was over.

"You're right. I just lost it for a second." Jamie was embarrassed that he'd let his emotions get out of control when he'd been ready to make love with Grant. "Sometimes when you're in my arms, I feel like it's just too good to be true. I'm fine. Could you just fuck me into oblivion here? I feel stupid for being so maudlin when we could be making love. Shut me up, please."

"Jamie?"

"Yeah?"

"Shut up." Grant leaned to cover Jamie's mouth, and Jamie gave it up completely. He flipped them over again, and they laughed and played for a few seconds.

Jamie got serious then and set about showing Grant how damned happy he was to have him in his life. He caressed every inch of Grant's body with fingertips, lips, and tongue. His heart began to beat harder, and his breathing was louder as he moved down to take Grant's hot, hard cock into his mouth and begin to lick it from base to tip. Grant jerked, his hand moving to lovingly cup the back of Jamie's head.

"Love your mouth on me, Jamie. So hot. So good," Grant moaned as he pushed up from the bed, forcing himself deeper into Jamie's mouth. Jamie just opened wider to make it easier. Grant began to move up and back, fucking Jamie's mouth while Jamie held the base of his cock, helping to guide him. With his mouth engaged, Jamie eased his other hand down to Grant's balls and behind to the crease between his buttocks. He heard Grant begin to pant as he got closer and closer to climax.

Grant stretched his arm way over to the bedside table for lube and a condom. He managed to grab them and lay them on the bed then was lost again to sensation as Jamie eased his finger inside his hole.

"Ahhh, God, Jamie. That feels so good." Jamie held on tight as Grant tried to spread for him, raising a leg to ease himself open a little more, making it easier for Jamie to work him. The combination of Jamie's mouth on his cock and his finger moving in and out slowly, had Grant nearly ready to blow. Jamie turned that long finger deep inside Grant and found that spot that had Grant jerking and shouting. Jamie touched it over and over as Grant shot great wads of cum into Jamie's waiting mouth. Jamie swallowed quickly, greedily taking his lover's essence.

Finally, Grant eased back down to the bed from the tight curl he'd been pulled into as he came. Jamie looked down at the satisfied look on Grant's face. He watched as Grant's head rolled a little and his eyes focused again. Jamie smiled down at him, smoothing his hand over Grant's chest, letting him have a few seconds to come down from his obvious high. Jamie was happy with his efforts. He liked feeling like he'd done that for Grant.

"Fuck me...now...please. Jamie, you've melted me, you've loved me, now just fuck me. Tell me how you want me."

"I'd love to fuck you on your hands and knees, but this time I want to watch your eyes the whole time." Jamie leaned to kiss Grant, sharing his own taste with him. "Love you, Grant." He reached for the slick and the condom, getting ready quickly.

Grant leaned up and reached to grab under his knees then rolled back slowly, making sure he could do it this way without his hip causing a problem. He smiled as he didn't feel but a small twinge. He looked up at Jamie and nodded at him, letting him know this was good. Jamie dipped his head, watching closely as he applied the lube to Grant's sweet hole. He covered himself and made sure he was good and slick, ready to take Grant the way they both needed.

He leaned and carefully placed the tip of his cock at Grant's exposed hole. He pushed slowly, and they both sighed as he eased inside. He kept his eyes on Grant's to make sure he wasn't causing him any pain in this position.

"It's good, baby, real good. Go on, fuck me like you want to. I'm fine, really."

That's what Jamie had needed. He pulled back and slammed in, still watching. When all Grant did was grin up at him, he knew it was okay. He set up a rhythm that had both of them grunting and moaning as he rammed into Grant over and over, staking the claim he'd needed to make. He never took his eyes off

Grant's. Grant seemed to know what this meant to Jamie. He just gave and gave, everything that Jamie needed.

"Love you, love you, love you." The litany continued each time Jamie slid inside Grant. Grant just looked up at him with the most beautiful smile Jamie had ever seen. He felt it happening, coming up from his balls, tightening them, burning and aching as he let go after ramming home one more time. Jet after jet of thick cream filled the condom as Jamie held still, deep inside Grant.

Jamie reached down and eased out of Grant, holding onto the condom. He took care of it, reaching for one of the towels they'd taken to leaving on the little table by the bed. He cleaned himself and then smoothed the towel over Grant, clearing away the excess lubricant. At last, he lay down beside Grant and sighed deeply.

"I needed that," Grant said, softly.

"Yeah?"

"Jamie, I love you with all my heart. I'm not ever leaving you. I'll be careful and not take chances and you must promise me that you'll do the same. The only thing that will separate us is…the end of our lives. We'll work through everything else that life throws at us. I have faith in us…together. We're a perfect match." He snuggled into Jamie's waiting arms.

"A perfect match. I love you, too, Grant. That's what'll keep us together. Love, Grant."

"Yeah. Love, Jamie."

About the Author

AKM Miles loves reading the M/M genre and decided to write what she loves. Early authors, read years ago in this area, were not as much interested in love, storyline, and character development, as those that she has found recently. Thrilled with the new works, AKM set out to make a career in this field. You can expect there to be a happy ending every time. You can expect for the two to find each other and choose to be together fairly early on, and then face conflicts, trials, and experiences as a couple. AKM prefers that over going back and forth over whether the love is returned or not. She loves to throw children in the mix, along with pets and wacky and wonderful friends. Hopefully, readers will love the emotional love stories that fill her head and spill onto her computer.

AKM loves to hear from readers. You can find her contact information, website details and author profile page at http://www.total-e-bound.com.

Total-E-Bound Publishing

www.total-e-bound.com

Take a look at our exciting range of literagasmic™
erotic romance titles and discover pure quality
at Total-E-Bound.

Made in the USA